DISCARD

JY 06 '17

PENNYBAKER SCHOOL
IS HEADED FOR DISASTER

Also by Jennifer Brown

Life on Mars

How Lunchbox Jones Saved Me from Robots,
Traitors, and Missy the Cruel

PENNYBAKER SCHOOL
IS HEADED FOR DISASTER

Jennifer Brown

illustrated by Marta Kissi

BLOOMSBURY

NEW YORK LONDON OXFORD NEW DELHI SYDNEY

First published in the United States of America in July 2017
by Bloomsbury Children's Books
www.bloomsbury.com

Bloomsbury is a registered trademark of Bloomsbury Publishing Plc

For information about permission to reproduce selections from this book, write to
Permissions, Bloomsbury Children's Books, 1385 Broadway, New York, New York 10018
Bloomsbury books may be purchased for business or promotional use. For information
on bulk purchases please contact Macmillan Corporate and Premium Sales Department
at specialmarkets@macmillan.com

Library of Congress Cataloging-in-Publication Data
Names: Brown, Jennifer, author.
Title: Pennybaker School is headed for disaster / by Jennifer Brown.
Description: New York : Bloomsbury, 2017.
Identifiers: LCCN 2016037702 (hardcover) • LCCN 2016049507 (e-book)
ISBN 978-1-68119-174-4 (hardcover) • ISBN 978-1-68119-175-1 (e-book)
Subjects: | CYAC: Gifted children—Fiction. | Boarding schools—Fiction. |
Schools—Fiction. | Friendship—Fiction. | Detective and mystery stories. |
BISAC: JUVENILE FICTION / Humorous Stories. | JUVENILE FICTION /
School & Education. | JUVENILE FICTION / Social Issues / Friendship.
Classification: LCC PZ7.B814224 Pan 2017 (print) | LCC PZ7.B814224 (ebook) |
DDC [Fic]—dc23
LC record available at https://lccn.loc.gov/2016037702

Book design by Colleen Andrews
Typeset by Westchester Book Composition
Printed and bound in the U.S.A. by Berryville Graphics Inc., Berryville, Virginia
2 4 6 8 10 9 7 5 3 1

All papers used by Bloomsbury Publishing, Inc., are natural, recyclable products
made from wood grown in well-managed forests. The manufacturing processes
conform to the environmental regulations of the country of origin.

To all my unique readers.
What makes you different is indeed a gift.
Now, go put on your reading socks!

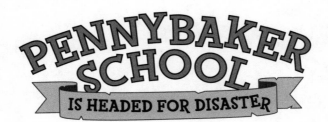

TRICK #1

THE SECOND HEAD ILLUSION

Louis XIV was my mortal enemy.

Sure, he was the beloved Sun King, and sure, he was artistic and stuff, and all the paintings show he had pretty great hair.

But he was also the first guy to wear a tie.

Okay, maybe not technically the first. Technically, Chinese emperor Qin Shi Huang had his soldiers wear them to command respect. And maybe some Romans might have worn kerchiefs around their necks to keep their vocal cords warm, because Romans were all persnickety about things like talking fancy. And, okay, some seventeenth-century Croatian warriors wore something like a necktie. Which was how a certain king with pretty great hair found out about them.

But Louis XIV was the first guy to wear a necktie just

because he liked the way it looked. He thought they were fashionable. Clearly, the dude had his kerchief tied just a little too tight.

As I stood in front of the bathroom mirror, hopelessly winding a scratchy brown strip of sandpapery fabric around my neck every which way but the correct one, I thought about the ways I could get revenge on Louis XIV for this torture, if he were not already dead:

Lethal duel with a broom handle. Toothpaste squirted in his Oreos. Smelly sauerkraut in his underwear drawer.

There was a knock on the door, and then it popped open, my dad's face peeking through.

"Nervous, pal?"

I pulled one end of the bow tie, and the whole thing knotted itself into a ball on the side of my neck. Half of my collar was flipped up, and if I squinted one eye just right, the tie-ball looked like a rat peeking out from under it. It was as close to tied as it was going to get. "Why would I be nervous?"

"New school, new friends." He sipped his coffee, then pointed at my neck with his cup. "New bow tie."

"No big deal," I said.

But it was a big deal. A very big deal. Such a big deal, in fact, that Louis Pennybaker was now a close number two on my mortal enemies list.

Bludgeoned with a salami hunk. Hospital glove slap-fight. Green pudding up the nostrils.

Louis Pennybaker was the founder of Pennybaker School for the Uniquely Gifted—which, it turns out, is where they send you when they start thinking you have unique gifts. For example, if you were a—to quote my mom—Chemistry Genius Who Will Change the World and Probably Discover a Whole Bunch of New Diseases and Then Cure Them All and May Invent a Species and Possibly Even Prove That UFOs Are Real by Using His Genius Geniusness. Exclamation point.

Actually, I was a kid who kind of liked magic tricks and figured out how to change pennies into silver. Except not real silver. It was a chemical reaction between copper, zinc, and sodium hydroxide to make them look silver. Which took me a long time to explain to Mom. She was very excited about the silver. So excited that I decided not to even show her that I could turn the silver ones into gold. She'd probably have enrolled me in college right then and there. Chemistry College for the Disease-Curing-Species-Creating-Alien-Proving-World-Changing Geniuses Who Can Make Gold.

Instead, she enrolled me at Pennybaker School. Because, apparently, my old school "doesn't have the resources" to "support such talent," and Pennybaker is "a really respected school" that would "look great on a résumé someday." Besides, "It's on the way to Dad's work," so he could drive me to school every day, and "it would be a great father-son bonding thing," and she "just likes the idea" of me "getting the best education possible" for *someone like me,* whatever that was supposed to mean. And Mom "always wished" that she had "gone to such an illustrious school," and, no, she didn't "think it was a funny suggestion" that she pretend to be me and go to Pennybaker herself, and apparently that was "the end of it, Thomas, so you should drop it before you get yourself in trouble with all that sass." To paraphrase.

The short version: I was going to Pennybaker School, period.

Which I was not at all excited about.

Going to a new school meant I'd have to leave my old school, where all my friends were, probably forgetting I ever existed. I would never get to fight for the one table in the Boone Public Middle School cafeteria that doesn't smell like an unfortunate, and perhaps even illegal, bologna incident. I would never get to try to top the legendary smuggled-armadillo-on-the-school-bus prank of 2002. And I would never get to have Mr. Butts, the computer lab teacher everyone wanted for obvious reasons.

"You need help with that tie?" Dad asked, gesturing with his cup again, a bit of brown liquid sailing over the side and landing on the sleeve of my crisp white uniform shirt.

"Nah, I think this is good," I said, and tried not to notice that the tie actually looked like a giant mole growing out of the side of my neck. Or possibly a second head. Which would be cool, if the head weren't made of scratchy brown material that came with a matching vest. I would have named the second head Louis XIV. And then tweezed out all his nose hairs.

Mortal nose tweezing.

"That's my man," Dad said. He reached in and patted my shoulder twice. "I'm headed to work. I'll want a full report tonight. Good luck."

"Thanks."

Dad disappeared, and soon Mom started hollering for me to hurry up or I'd be late for the first day of my "new adventure."

My mom called everything that was awful an "adventure." There was the "Dentist Coming at Your Face with a Power Tool Adventure" and the "Seven-Thousand-Needle Kindergarten Shots Adventure" and the "Boring Restaurant with Gross Froofy Food and Eyeballs on Your Plate Adventure" and the "Going to a New School Where They Wear Bow Ties Adventure." Mom needed to look up the definition of "adventure" again, because I was pretty sure she had absolutely no idea what an adventure really was.

Slowly, I put on my scratchy brown sandpaper vest. It buttoned around my stomach so tightly I didn't see how I would ever eat so much as a grape without feeling like a snake with a frog in its stomach. I could feel the itchy fiber all the way to my liver.

At Boone Public, we wore what we wanted. T-shirts. Jeans. Tennis shoes. At Pennybaker School, we wore brown

5

things and penny loafers. My mom thought putting a shiny penny in each shoe would be a clever way to let everyone know what my gift was. But, more important, it would make them look cute.

They weren't cute.

They were not a Penny Loafer Adventure.

"Hurry up, fish face," my little sister, Erma, said as she flitted past the bathroom. She crossed her eyes and sucked in her cheeks, moving her lips up and down like a fish does.

"Stuff it, Erma," I said.

"Only a turkey would say something like that," she said, then raced down the stairs, flapping her elbows and gobbling.

I rolled my eyes. Fifth graders were so annoying. There was no possible way that I had been that annoying just last year. Erma was jealous that she wasn't going to Pennybaker School with me. She really thought it was an actual adventure. Erma was very weird.

I pawed off the bathroom light and followed her down the stairs, my whole body feeling like it was filled with wet sand. Itchy, brown wet sand. And pennies.

"There he is," Mom said as I came into the kitchen. She placed a plate piled high with pancakes on the table next to a stack of bacon and a bowl filled with sliced oranges. "I was starting to worry. I don't want you to be late on your first day."

"I can get him there real fast on my motorcycle," Grandma Jo said.

"Mother, I told you, no more motorcycle," Mom said. She scooted her chair in between Erma and me.

"And I told you you'll have to pry my helmet out of my cold, dead hands," Grandma Jo said defiantly.

Mom crossed her arms, looking vexed. "Well, you're definitely not taking Thomas or Erma on that deathtrap."

Grandma Jo stuffed a bite of pancake into her mouth. "Old fuddy-duddy," she said.

Truth was, Grandma Jo was not the kind of grandma who needed a babysitter. Grandma Jo liked fast things on wheels and taking hot-wing challenges at restaurants. Grandma Jo was a twenty-year-old in a seventy-year-old's body. But try to tell Mom that. One day, about a month ago, Grandma Jo took a turn too narrowly on her bike, crashed into a parked car, and broke a wrist and two ribs. Three days later, we were moving Grandma Jo, and all her Grandma Jo stuff, into our house, even though Grandma Jo swore it was just a onetime accident and she didn't need any help. Mom was an only child. She thought it was up to her to make sure Grandma Jo lived a long time. So Grandma Jo moved. And we all quickly learned that Grandma Jo liked having company, but she didn't like being told what to do.

Mom was very persistent, though. Grandma Jo didn't know this yet, but she was having a You're Never Riding Your Motorcycle Again Adventure.

"It's okay, Grandma," I said. "I'd rather not mess up my uniform with the wind anyway."

Grandma Jo looked me up and down, then stuffed another bite of pancake into her mouth and harrumphed, shrugging.

"What did you do to your tie?" Mom asked.

I glanced down. "Tied it."

"With your feet, maybe," Erma said. I made a face at her; she made one back at me. I flicked a hunk of bacon at her; she squealed like I'd tossed a vat of boiling bat guts at her, then started whining at Mom, which was what Erma did best.

"Okay," Mom said. "That's enough of that. Finish up and get your backpacks. Thomas, your tie is . . . fine." But she didn't look convinced.

That made two of us.

Erma sprang up from her chair and raced for her room, and Grandma toddled over to the coffeepot to refill her mug.

"Oh, here, let me help you with that," Mom said to Grandma Jo, lunging for the coffeepot. Grandma Jo swatted at her with a dish towel, and they started squabbling over whether or not Grandma Jo could pour a cup of coffee by herself.

Leaving me to myself and my pancake.

Which had taken on a funny shape. Double chin. Fluffy hair. Upturned nose. Fancy-guy cravat.

I pressed the back of my fork into it, watching the syrup pool in the ridges. *Aha! Stuck to death in a swamp of syrup. Almost too good for you, Louis XIV.*

"Come on, Thomas," Mom called from the counter, where she was grabbing her keys and purse. "Time's up."

"Right," I said.

I got up and yanked hard on the brown tie-wad, which only got tighter as I pulled, like a boa constrictor made out of wool.

Maybe not too good for you after all, Louis.

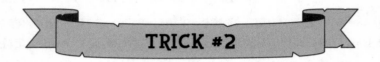

TRICK #2

POOF! AN ACTOR APPEARS!

"It leans to the left," I said as Mom pulled into the circular driveway in front of Pennybaker School.

"So tilt your head to the right," she said. As if that could solve anything. As if I could bend my neck with this tie on anyway. I would probably pass out from lack of oxygen.

Which might be a good thing, if it meant I would get sent home from the illustrious Pennybaker School for the Uniquely Gifted. Blah.

"Isn't it beautiful?" Mom said, craning her neck to look at the upper floors.

"Beautiful" must be right next to "adventure" in Mom's dictionary.

To me, Pennybaker School looked terrible. All brick,

rows of windows like evil, glaring eyes covered with ivy eyebrows—green plants that climbed all the way up the front and even over the roof, making the building look angry and alive.

Pennybaker School was founded by Louis Pennybaker in 1895. Once a one-room schoolhouse built on the outskirts of town, it had been built up and built out over the years until it was a looming building sprawling over the top of the tallest hill in Clair County like a big, ugly hat. Or a giant fanged spidermonster protecting its nest.

Even from the parking lot of Boone Public, which was all the way on the other side of town, you could see Pennybaker School staring down at you with its hundreds of spidermonster eyes, demanding that you notice and appreciate it. Students at Pennybaker School had a reputation for being studious, kind of mysterious, and definitely well mannered. Translation: snooty-patootey.

"Do you want me to walk you in?" Mom asked.

I watched as a group of giggling girls walked up the front steps. A pack of guys met with high fives on the sidewalk. Some stragglers peered curiously into our car. The last thing I needed was to be the new kid who got walked into middle school by his mommy.

"No, I got it," I said. "I'll figure out where to go."

"Okay," Mom said, and then she gave me the wobbly

smile thing that moms do when they're getting ready to get squishy on you. "My baby. You're so brave."

I knew it. Super squish.

"Thanks, Mom. I don't want to be late," I said. I pecked her on the cheek and then plunged out into the crowd.

The very scary crowd filled with properly tied brown bow ties.

I waited until Mom pulled away, then took a deep breath and marched toward the front doors, which I now noticed had snarling gray metal lion heads on them. The kind that are always, 100 percent of the time, on doors in horror movies featuring haunted mansions that people go into and never come out of. There was no way I was reaching for that door. In horror movies, it never turns out well for the guy who reaches for the door.

"Excuse me! Excuse me! Young man!" I heard. A frazzled-looking woman was hurrying across the lawn toward me, the sleeves of her dress billowing in the breeze as she lifted her arm to wave. "Excuse me!"

I started toward her, relieved to be away from the lion heads. I'm not proud to admit it, but I was totally willing to let her be the one to reach for the door first.

"Hello, hello," the woman said as she got closer. "You must be our new student, Thomas Fallgrout." I nodded. She was out of breath from her race across the lawn. "I've been watching for an unfamiliar face. I'm Miss Munch.

The school secretary. I'm supposed to help you get started. Follow me."

I had so many questions, but Miss Munch was surprisingly fast, whipping open the doors as if the lions weren't even there. I practically had to jog to keep up as we plowed our way through the crowd of kids in the foyer. I tried not to notice the curious stares.

"Good morning, Miss Munch," a girl said as we passed. "Your dress is really pretty today."

Miss Munch paused long enough to curtsy, then we were off again. "Thank you, Cecily," she said over her shoulder. Then to me, "Cecily is such a lovely girl. You'd never know about the chain saws."

"Chain saws?" I looked back at the girl, who was small and fragile and seemed way too girly to have the words "chain saws" in the same sentence as her name.

"She juggles them," Miss Munch said lightly. "Well, not just chain saws. Knives, battle-axes, flaming sticks. And once, live possums. She's very good, actually. One might say she's uniquely gifted." Miss Munch giggled. "Oh, that joke never gets old."

The foyer of the Pennybaker School for the Uniquely Gifted was a big circle filled with stained glass and a ceiling that went all the way up to the top floor. A staircase wound its way around and around, and was filled with kids racing to get to their classes, making me dizzy as I tried to watch them. The marble floor was so shiny it looked like a mirror, and right in the center of the foyer was a giant pedestal.

And on top of the pedestal was a head.

It was bronze with wild frizzy hair, bulging eyes, and a mouth open in a scream. Like a gargoyle, only worse. It was the scariest thing I'd ever experienced, and that included the first night after Grandma Jo moved in, when I almost drank her false teeth.

Miss Munch must have seen me staring at the head.

"Oh," she said. "That's Helen."

"You named your scary head Helen?"

"Helen Heirmauser," she said. "Beloved math teacher of many years. Practically everyone in town had Mrs. Heirmauser for their teacher." She gazed reverently at the statue. "Or wanted to. Even those who didn't have her felt like they had. Including people who never attended this school. They say she even taught Louis Pennybaker himself in the eighteen hundreds."

I counted years in my head. "I don't think that's possible."

"She was pretty old when she died."

"She died?"

Miss Munch knelt in front of the pedestal, placing her hand over her heart and bowing her head. "And the whole town shut down for an entire week." She stayed like that for so long that I started to feel weird and began to kneel down next to her. But the second my knee touched the floor, Miss Munch wiped the corners of her eyes with her fingertips and stood up, leaving me kneeling there by myself with my hands pressed together like I was praying. Two girls walked by, looked at me, and giggled.

"Now, this way, please," Miss Munch said, completely unaware of my humiliation, and we were off again.

We walked around the statue, past a window occupied by a woman who was talking on the phone, and through a door into the office.

"Just let me get your schedule," Miss Munch said. "Wait right here." She gestured toward a bench that was currently occupied by a very small boy with glasses and a much bigger boy who kept staring at my tie-wad. I wished I had let Dad help me with my tie. I decided not to sit.

Miss Munch moved behind the big secretary desk. She wiggled the computer mouse and tapped a few keys.

"Miss Munch?" the tiny boy said tentatively.

She glanced up. "Yes, Flea?"

"I forgot my didgeridoo. I called my mom. She's bringing it. But I might need a late pass."

Miss Munch got a crease between her eyebrows. "This is the third time this month," she said.

The boy stood, coming up to about my shoulder. "I'm sorry, Miss Munch. I won't forget again, I promise. But if I don't have it, Mr. Flugel's whole concert will go down the tubes."

"Well, I certainly doubt the entire concert rests on one didgeridoo, Flea."

"But I'm the *only* didgeridoo," the boy complained.

"Actually, when played right, the didgeridoo is quite the commanding presence on stage, both because of its intimidating size and its soothing buzzing sound." The larger boy with the perfect tie had stood up. His voice boomed through the office, clear and commanding and slightly Australian.

"Thank you, Wesley," Miss Munch said, looking irritated, before going back to the computer.

"Of course, mate," he said, bowing with a flourish and sitting down again.

I tried to piece together what I'd just heard, but none of it made sense. Flea? Mr. Flugel? And what the heck was a didgeridoo, anyway?

"Okay," Miss Munch finally said, moving over to catch a piece of paper as it came out of the printer. "You should be all set, Thomas."

She brought me the paper and smiled. I took it and read the names of my classes.

1st period: Biofeedback
2nd period: Active Numbering
3rd period: Four Square
4th period: Lexiconical Arts
5th period: Meat and Greet Gathering
6th period: Claymaking
7th period: Futuristic Arts
8th period: Facts After the Fact

"I don't understand these," I said, letting the paper droop. The bell rang. Miss Munch put her hand on my shoulder.

"Don't worry, Wesley is going to explain everything to you. He's your Pennybaker School ambassador."

The taller boy stood and bowed again, then pulled an old-fashioned white hanky out of his pocket and waved it around between two fingers like some dude in an opera. "At jor zervice, zir," he said, but he said it in a funny voice. An entirely not-Australian voice.

"What?"

"I repeat. At yuh suhvice, suh." Another different accent. But at least this one was an accent I understood. British, maybe. Or he had a stuffy nose. I couldn't tell. It was allergy season, after all.

Just then, a tiny woman burst into the office, dragging an instrument case that was twice her size.

"Oh! Perfect timing! I might still get to class on time," the boy named Flea yelped. He jumped up, took the instrument, and staggered out the door, dragging the case behind him just as the woman had been doing. The door banged into him twice before he finally got all the way out. Miss Munch had her eyes closed and her fingers pressed to her temples.

"Let me just write you two some passes," she said. "So you don't have to hurry to class." She bustled back to her desk and whipped out a pad of paper. "That way you can chat. And you, Thomas, can ask all the questions you need to ask." Oh, I doubted there was enough time for that.

Wesley leaned over my schedule. "Biofeedback is meditation class," he said. "It's supposed to be science. But everyone just sleeps. We call it nap class."

"What about these others?" I asked.

He frowned, then went down the list. "Math, gym, English, the usual," he said, pointing at my second-, third-, and fourth-period classes.

"Meat and greet?"

He smiled, then growled in a monster voice that made my hair fly back off my forehead and rattled my tie-ball, "LUNCH." And then he added in a totally normal voice, "And then art. And computers. Which is taught by Mr. Püp."

Seriously? Butts and now Püp? What were the odds?

Miss Munch came back, brandishing two pink slips for us. "Okay, you're good to go."

"Shall we?" The British accent again.

I followed Wesley into the hall, which was filled with only a smattering of kids now, all racing to get to class.

"So as youse can see, we gots a pretty intricate operation going on around heres," he said in a gangster voice.

I'd had about enough. "Okay, what's with all the accents?" I asked. "Does everyone here do that?"

Wesley gathered himself up tall. "Only we thessssspians."

About a gallon of spit drenched my forehead. I needed windshield wipers.

"What's a thespian?" I asked, drying my forehead with

my schedule. I didn't know why I kept asking questions—every time I asked one, I just ended up more confused.

"You know," Wesley said. "An actor. Someone who loves the theater. We thespians never miss an opportunity to practice portrayal. Life is art. Art is life. Plus, auditions for *Annie* are coming up, and I've always thought Daddy Warbucks needed an accent. How do you feel about a Slovakian inflection?"

I stared at him for a long time. He never said "just kidding" or started laughing, so he must have been serious. "Okay."

We walked past the head in the foyer and I shuddered.

"You've met Mrs. Heirmauser, I presume?" Wesley said, pausing only long enough to place his hand over his heart and gaze at the head with reverence.

"Why does she look like that?" I asked.

"Like what?"

"You know." I made a buggy-eyed face and opened my mouth wide, rabid dog–style.

"Oh," he said. "She was passionate about math."

He started up the stairs, and I trailed behind him. "What does that mean?"

He paused and thought about it. "She yelled a lot," he said over his shoulder, then kept walking. "But it was a loving yell."

"Loving yell," I repeated, casting one last look at the head. It didn't look so loving. Or maybe it did—loving in the way a lion loves a nice, juicy goat.

The bell rang, and all around us we could hear shoes frantically scuffling and classroom doors shutting.

"Zoinks! We should hurry," Wesley said, in what was clearly a cartoon voice. "We have to get all the way to the top."

I turned my eyes to the ceiling, which seemed impossibly far away. Like we might need an airplane to get there. We walked for what seemed like forever, Wesley occasionally breaking out into show tunes, each of which he seemed to know only a few words of. My legs were killing me, and my necktie-clump had begun to shrink. My vest popped a button. It plinked down the stairs all the way to the foyer. Sweat trickled down my back, making it itch even more. I wasn't sure how I was going to do this every single morning.

Finally, we reached the top.

"Your second-period class is right down the hall," Wesley said. "I have that one, too, so I'll help you find it. Enjoy your biofeedback." He took a deep breath in through his nose and let it out through his mouth, yoga-style. "Ommm," he said, then let out a loud snore. I had no clue what he was doing, but I was too exhausted to ask. He opened his eyes, smiled, punched me lightly on the shoulder, and said, "See ya!"

"Wait," I said. He stopped. I pointed to my schedule. "You didn't tell me what my eighth-hour class is. Facts After the Fact?"

"Oh." Wesley brightened. "That's history. Right now we're studying Louis XIV."

And then he was gone.

Death by history class.

TRICK #3

FLYING SALIVA PAPER

It turned out Wesley was in most of my classes. Which was good, because, as strange as the accents and stuff were, he was a pretty nice guy. And a guy who suddenly sings the girl parts of *High School Musical* songs for no reason whatsoever is a guy who definitely isn't going to judge someone if they do something embarrassing.

Not that anyone at Pennybaker School would notice if I did something embarrassing—of that I was becoming certain. Seemed everyone in the school was a little bit off. Boys who spoke through ventriloquist dummies, girls who unicycled, teachers who wore ball gowns and clog danced in the middle of the lesson. And every four minutes, someone made a reference to the Great Helen Heirmauser, and the whole class would turn, hands over their hearts, and look toward the foyer, where the creepy, screaming, eye-buggy head was. God rest her soul. Or whatever.

In Lexiconical Arts, a girl who wore black clothes under her uniform and a black beret on her head recited a poem she'd written for the Heirmauser bust:

Ode to the great Helen Heirmauser
Who always had a crease on the legs of her trouser
If she were a cat, she'd be a great mouser
And if she were a dog, she'd be better than a
*   schnauzer*
She always made math not boring but wowser
And she knew more answers than an Internet
*   search engine.*

"Sorry," she said to Mrs. Codex. "I couldn't think of anything to rhyme on that last one."

Mrs. Codex blinked. "How about 'Internet browser'?"

"Oh, good point," said the girl in black. "I should search for a rhyme on an Internet browser."

"No," said Mrs. Codex. "'Browser' rhymes with 'Heirmauser.'"

The girl smiled wide, nodding. "What a coincidence, huh? I'll bet that's a good-luck sign that I'll find the perfect word."

"No, no," said Mrs. Codex. Her neck had started to turn red.

"She means a browser and an Internet search engine are the same thing," the boy named Flea piped from the back of the room.

The girl in black looked very confused.

"Not exactly true," said a boy near the window. He had three computers on his desk, all open to different webpages. He also had a smartphone, a very complicated-looking watch, and, most interestingly, an upside-down spaghetti strainer on his head. He consulted a page on one of the computers. "Technically, a browser is what you have to open to get to a search engine."

"Close enough," said Flea.

The boy scratched his head under the spaghetti strainer and tapped a few keys on one of the computers, then input something into his phone. "Well, I suppose if Clara wants to be *close enough* in her poem written about our greatest teacher of all time." The entire class paused, pressed their hands to their hearts, and gazed toward the door, which looked out upon the foyer. And the head. I sighed and tried really hard not to roll my eyes.

The girl in black, who I'd now deduced was named Clara, looked stricken. "Oh, goodness, I don't want that at all!"

"I didn't think so," the boy said. "I can find you a rhyming word on Google—which is a search engine, by the way."

"Aha! I've got it!" Clara, beaming, leaned over Mrs. Codex's desk, erased furiously, wrote a few words, and then stood up proudly to read.

Ode to the great Helen Heirmauser
Who always had a crease on the legs of her trouser
If she were a cat, she'd be a great mouser
And if she were a dog, she'd be better than a
   schnauzer
She always made math not boring but wowser
And she knew more answers than Google.

Mrs. Codex looked like she was going to throw up.

7

The class I was least looking forward to was the last one, where I had a sinking feeling I was about to have a Louis XIV Boring Torturous Lecture Adventure. I was also pretty sure I had a raging rash under my tie and my vest, and somehow both had managed to get tighter, even though I'd probably sweated off half my body weight. I felt like I was wrapped inside a live beaver. The last thing I wanted to do was spend an entire hour talking about the man who started it all.

Louis XIV: Gnawed to death by a live beaver.

Wesley and I took seats in the very back row.

"Don't worry. Mr. Faboo is an easy grader," Wesley
"And he really gets into history. He even has costun
Sometimes he forgets we're here at all. Which is why .
brought . . ." He pulled two straws out of his backpack and
held them up.

"What's that?" I asked.

He ripped two sheets of paper out of his spiral notebook
and handed one to me. "Boredom buster." He tore a small
scrap off one corner and tucked it into his mouth, chewing
around a grin. After a few moments, he stuck out his tongue,
a perfectly round, extraordinarily spitty spitwad perched on
the end. He plucked it off his tongue and stuffed it into the
end of the straw. *Now watch,* he mouthed, holding up one
finger. I watched.

"We have a new project to discuss today, class," Mr.
Faboo said. "A very exciting new project. I think you will like
this one a lot." He turned and picked up a marker, which
had a giant feather taped to the end like an old-timey quill.
He started writing on the board, and that was when Wesley
let the spitwad rip.

Patoo!

The white ball sailed through the air, expertly skimming
the very tops of our classmates' heads, and found its home
in the back of Mr. Faboo's hair, which sproinged lightly as
the paper landed. Mr. Faboo paused, scratched his head, and

27

went back to writing. Twenty pairs of eyes turned to stare at Wesley and me incredulously. I gulped and turned to Wesley, who had already hidden his straw and was studiously scribbling away in his spiral notebook, as if he were taking notes. The tiniest of grins touched the corners of his mouth.

I looked back and realized everyone was actually just staring at me.

Because I was still holding my straw.

My face burned and I looked down, giving myself a bowtie mustache.

"Nationwide History Day," Mr. Faboo cried, and everyone turned back toward him, as if nothing had just happened. "You are to research and study any history subject and create a multimedia presentation regarding said subject. For example, you might gather and present Native American artifacts or make a movie about Henry Kissinger."

I glanced at Wesley again. He was laughing so hard he was crying. "Your turn," he whispered.

"You're crazy," I whispered back. A bead of sweat disappeared down my back and into my underwear.

"He'll never know," Wesley said.

"No way."

"What, are you a chicken?" He *bawk*ed softly.

"Shut up!"

"Excuse me, young man," Mr. Faboo said, and once again

I felt the eyes of the entire class on me. My face burned even harder, and more sweat rolled down my back. Great. Now I was having a Sitting in Sweat Pond Adventure. "Excuse me. Have we met?"

I shook my head. "I'm new," I said.

"And you're called?"

"I'm sorry?"

"What is your name?"

"Oh. Thomas. Fallgrout. Thomas Fallgrout."

Mr. Faboo tickled his chin with the feather. "Tell me, Thomas Fallgrout, Thomas Fallgrout. Have you an idea for the Nationwide History Day project?"

"Um . . ." No. All that my brain could think was, *Spitwad spitwad there's a spitwad in your hair spitwad spitty spitty spitwad*. How could I think of anything historical with all that spitty wadiness right there for all to see?

Mr. Faboo looked unimpressed. "Well, new student Thomas Fallgrout, Thomas Fallgrout," he said, "I suppose you should do less talking and more thinking, then." He turned back to the board. All the eyes followed him.

All except Wesley's, which were pointed directly at me.

"I know ye've got it in ya, laddy," he whispered in an Irish brogue.

I didn't. At least Thomas Fallgrout from Boone Public Middle School didn't. But I wasn't at Boone Public Middle School anymore, was I? I was sitting in Lake Buttsweat, getting yelled at in front of everyone by a guy who talked all old-fashioned and fancy like . . . like Louis XIV.

My eyes narrowed. Maybe Thomas Fallgrout from Boone Public didn't have it in him, but Thomas Fallgrout from Pennybaker School did.

I swallowed, my whole body tingling with adrenaline.

I tore a piece of paper and stuck it into my mouth, chewing quickly, feeling my chin bump the tie-ball with every chew.

This is what I think of you, Louis XIV, I thought, then stuffed the spitwad into the straw, brought it up to my lips, and blew.

Direct hit.

Mr. Faboo scratched his head again. Twenty pairs of eyes glared at me. Wesley low-fived me under the desk.

"Man," Wesley said as we tumbled out of the classroom forty-five minutes later. "You really nailed him with that last one. Are you, like, a spitball master or something?"

I grinned, loosening my tie and letting the ends of it dangle against my chest. I felt like I could breathe for the first time all day. "I'm pretty great with a Nerf gun, but this is my first weapon of slobberatic destruction."

"Well, you could have fooled me. I've never seen a first-timer do so good. You'll be a great addition to the team."

We'd turned the corner and joined the crowd jogging down the stairs, around and around and around, like cars stuck in a traffic circle. I wondered if I'd ever be able to get to a class without feeling dizzy.

"What team?"

We reached the second floor, and Wesley took my arm and pulled me into the hallway. A button popped off my vest. Someone kicked it down the stairs—*plink, plink, plink.* Two buttons down, two left, and it was only the first day. Soon my vest would be hanging open, which was probably against a billion Pennybaker School rules and would make fancy Louis XIV want to croak.

Fashion faux pas fatality.

Wesley led me into a little alcove where there was a closet. It was dark and creepy, the fluorescent light above our heads buzzing.

"There's this thing," Wesley whispered. He paused, licked his lips, and looked around. "The Annual Boys Versus Girls Pennybaker School Spitwad War. We have it every October. Dates all the way back to . . . well, this is the first year. But I've heard boys have been wanting to spit wads of paper at girls for a long time now. At least as far back as the cavemen."

"Cavemen? Did they have paper? And straws?" I asked, and Wesley shushed me, clamping a palm over my mouth. He gave me a meaningful look and took his hand away. "Why are we whispering?" I asked.

Again with the looks. You would think, by the way he was acting, that Wesley was about to tell me where he'd buried treasure. Or a body.

"If Nurse Hale finds out about it, she'll get all 'keep your saliva to yourselves' and call our moms. And then we'll have to watch that video about germs and snot and stuff in health class again."

"And what does this have to do with me, exactly?"

Wesley put his arm around my shoulders. "You're a natural, man. You have magic aim. You could probably even take out Abigail Thew, and she's being scouted by the Olympics for shotput. The girl can throw. But you, my friend, can spit."

"I got lucky," I said.

"No! Never say that. You're gifted, Thomas Fallgrout."

I rolled my eyes. "So I hear. It's my supposed giftedness that got me put here."

Wesley nodded and gave my shoulder three hearty whacks. "Just clear out your calendar. October. We haven't announced a date yet. Makes it harder for Nurse Hale to crack a fella if he doesn't know the date." He sniffed loudly and wiped his nose with one finger—his gangster persona.

"Whatever you say," I said. We headed back toward the stairs, which had emptied out.

"So what is your gift?" he asked.

"Huh?"

His eyebrows waggled up and down. "You know, your unique skill. Why are you here?"

"Oh. That." I thought for a second, then pulled off my tie. I held it up with one hand, then put my hands together. When I pulled them apart, the tie had disappeared. "Alacazam," I mumbled, slipping the "disappeared" tie into my back pocket with my free hand while I showed him the palm of the other hand.

Wesley's eyes grew big. "Whoa! You're a magician?"

I shrugged. "Not really. I guess. More like an alchemist. No. Yes. I don't know."

Truth was, I'd never thought of myself as a magician or a scientist, and certainly not as a genius. I was just a kid who had a Grandpa Rudy trunk.

Grandpa Rudy was the real magician. Well, not a famous one or anything. Just the kind people hired for their kids' birthday parties and stuff. "Rudy the Resplendent" was what he called himself. He had a cape and a top hat and everything. And a rabbit named Bill, but Bill hopped away during a show at a nursing home, and Grandpa Rudy was so upset he never replaced him.

Grandpa Rudy was cool. I used to watch him practice for his shows.

And I got to see how all the tricks were done.

When Grandpa Rudy died, Grandma Jo gave me his magician trunk. She figured I was the only one who would want it. It was mostly full of junk—rings with splits in them that you could barely see, old decks of cards, strings with knots, moldy rabbit food, and a dish with the word "Bill" on the side.

But inside the trunk, under all the bric-a-brac, under his cape and even under his top hat, was another box. A box full of jars with letters like "NaOH" and "Na_2CO_3" and "$C_2H_3NaO_2$" taped onto the sides of them. There were also a tape recorder and three cassettes full of Grandpa Rudy himself talking about his growing interest in science tricks, how he thought he was perfecting something new and exciting, and instructions on how to use the powders and liquids in the jars.

I missed Grandpa Rudy. A lot. And I listened to those cassettes about a gazillion times. And after listening to them about a gazillion times, I suddenly knew how to turn pennies silver. And gold.

So, in a way, it was Grandpa Rudy's fault that I was at Pennybaker School for the Uniquely Gifted with a sweaty brown bow tie in my back pocket.

"Make something else disappear," Wesley was saying as we headed down the stairs.

"Nah," I said.

"Make my tie disappear. Go ahead. Do it."

"Maybe later."

"Make this handrail disappear. My backpack. Make my backpack disappear. Oh, I know, make my homework disappear."

I pulled the bow tie out of my back pocket and dangled it before him. "Abracadabra," I said. "It was in my pocket the whole time."

Wesley stopped. "I thought magicians weren't supposed to tell how they do their tricks."

"That's what makes me not a magician," I said. "I just had a Grandpa Rudy."

Wesley's eyes brightened. "Hey, I have one of those, too! Except it's an uncle. My grandpa's name is Lou."

We'd reached the bottom of the stairs. I could see Mom's car through the front doors. I started toward it.

"Wait," Wesley said. I turned back impatiently. "You forgot." He gestured toward the Heirmauser head with its rolly eyes and screaming mouth.

"Forgot what?"

He dropped to one knee, hand over his heart, head bowed. "May we always be mathly motivated the Heirmauser way," he said in a sincere voice.

"Creepy," I muttered.

"Huh?" Wesley asked, getting to his feet.

I bent my knees, acting as if I were just getting up, too. "I said, 'Amen.'"

He squinted at me. "Nobody says that. That would be weird."

"Right," I said.

I would hate to make bowing to a bronze head weird, after all.

TRICK #4

A CHIP IN A TRACHTEN HAT

Chip Mason was on his front porch when I got home.

I slid down in my seat so my eyes were level with the door handle as Mom pulled into the driveway.

"What are you doing?" Mom asked.

"Just drive," I said. "Act natural. Don't look at me. Pull into the garage. Circle the neighborhood. Drive to the grocery store. Just do . . . something."

"Why on earth . . . You're acting strange, Thomas, and after your grandmother's stunt today, I don't have the patience for strange. Did you know I had to take her Rollerblades away from her? Again? Rollerblades. At her age. Can you believe that?"

Actually, yes, I could absolutely believe that. In fact, I wouldn't be surprised if Grandma Jo had been planning to use the Rollerblades to skate to a skydiving field. Come to think of it, Grandma Jo would have probably been a perfect fit for Pennybaker School for the Uniquely Gifted. Grandma Jo's unique gift would be trying to get away with stuff she shouldn't be doing.

But Mom would never see that as a gift. She would never think Grandma Jo was an Adventurer Genius Who Would Change the World of Daredevils Forever. She would never get behind Grandma Jo's Rollerblading Adventure.

"I swear, I just don't know what I'm going to do with that woman. Oh, look, there's that sweet boy across the street." Mom rolled down her window and leaned out. I pulled the lever on the side of my seat and flopped backward, closing my eyes and groaning. "Hello, Chip! What luck—Thomas is just getting home. I'm sure he'd love to play. Sit up, Thomas. I don't know what's gotten into you. I'm thinking a little fresh air might do you some good. Don't you want to play with Chip?"

No. On so many levels, no.

First, no matter how many times I tried to explain to Mom, she would never understand that in middle school, a dude doesn't *play*. He *hangs out*. He *gets together*. He *chills with his buddies*. Play? Never. Unless, of course, we actually were playing something. Like football or basketball. Or a board game. Or, I guess, technically, a play. But we wouldn't be out there putting on a play. We certainly wouldn't be playing a play. Unless the play was about playing football or basketball or a board game. Then I guess maybe you could say we were playing in a play while we were playing. It was a very complicated system.

But the bigger reason I didn't want to play with Chip Mason was Chip Mason.

He was weird. And, trust me, if a kid wearing a brown vest and a second-head bow tie who spent half the day bowing to a bronze screaming head thinks another kid is weird, that kid is capital-"W" weird.

Chip Mason moved in across the street a few months ago. Technically, he and his mom moved in with the guy who already lived there—Old Huck Mason—who, it turned out, was Chip's grandfather, and who, according to Grandma Jo, invented cranky. Mom said Old Huck was sick, and Chip and his mom were there to take care of him.

At first I was excited to get a new neighbor. Our neighborhood had no kids my age, which was why my best friends were a recording of my grandfather's voice and a magic top hat. But the minute I met Chip Mason, I knew the top hat and I were going to stay buddies for a long, long time.

The first time I saw Chip Mason, he was standing next to the big moving truck in his driveway in a tuxedo shirt, gym shorts, and furry purple socks that crept up his legs like caterpillars, ending just above his knees. His feet were poked into regular old tennis shoes, as if it were nothing to wear regular old tennis shoes with socks like that. Actually . . . I wasn't exactly sure what the appropriate shoe choice for socks like that would be.

"Greetings, native!" Chip said, waving with his whole arm. "I bring good tidings from the faraway lands of Long Field Middle. What say you regarding the atmosphere of this glad town? Any pertinent news or information? How hails my soon-to-be alma mater, Boone Public Middle School?"

"What?" I asked looking up, because "atmosphere" was pretty much the only word he'd said that I understood, but I didn't see anything unusual in the sky. "It's cloudy," I ventured, and then said what was really on my mind. "Why are you wearing fur socks?"

He came across the street. "These," he gestured toward his feet, "are my vocabulary socks."

"Vocabulary what?"

He looked baffled, as if I had just crawled out from under a rock, moss hanging from my nose. "You don't have vocabulary socks?"

I shook my head. Most of me was sure this Chip Mason kid was crazy, but I'll admit, part of me was wondering if maybe I was supposed to have vocabulary socks. Like that time I was supposed to have black shorts for gym class and had to borrow a spare pair that made my underwear smell like cough drops for the whole rest of the day.

"That's okay," he said, smiling wide. "I'll tell you the word of the day myself." He pulled his foot up as high as it would go, cocked his head to listen, then nodded and looked up again. "The word of the day is 'schnitzel.' S-C-H-N-I-T-Z-E-L. Schnitzel. Used in a sentence, 'I think I will have a wiener schnitzel and a bowl of *graupensuppe* for lunch today.'"

I blinked. "Wiener schnitzel? Like, a hot dog?"

He poked a finger in the air. "It's a commonly held misconception that, due to the word 'wiener' in the name, a wiener schnitzel is some form of sausage link. But that's not true. A wiener schnitzel is actually a piece of veal, pounded thin, dredged in bread crumbs, and fried. Not a hot dog, which is good with ketchup and served on a bun. The wiener schnitzel is Austria's national dish. Not many people know that. Ironically, many would claim that the national dish of the United States is the hot dog." He laughed as if he'd said something funny.

"Are you calling me stupid?" I asked, because I didn't really understand anything he'd said, other than the "not many people know that" part, and I figured it was a fair bet that by "not many people," he meant me. "It's a little-known fact that Thomas Fallgrout is a stupid stupidhead," he might as well have said, if he'd known my name. "Stupidly doomed with stupidity for all stupid time." And something about hot dogs.

"Quite the contrary," the boy said. "I do not know your

intelligence quotient, and I am hardly a trained professional who could assess it in any case. But you seem to have all the hallmarks of a relatively intelligent young man."

"What?"

I was pretty sure that the sixth graders at Boone Public Middle School were going to eat Chip Mason alive on a bun with ketchup, and it turned out I was right. According to Chip, his "unwonted idiosyncrasies" made it difficult for his peers to fully relate to him. According to Mom, that meant other kids thought he was weird and pretty much stayed away from him. It was one thing to avoid a kid for fifty minutes in your science class; it was a lot more difficult to ward him off when he was your neighbor. Even though his "unwonted idiosyncrasies" made it difficult for me to relate to him, it seemed that, other than his grandfather Huck, I was Chip's only friend in the world.

Lucky me.

"*Sei gegrüßt*, neighbor!" Chip Mason called when I got out of the car after my first day at Pennybaker School. I gave Mom the evil eye, but she didn't seem to notice.

"Hey, Chip."

He raced across the street, his shiny black shoes making clunky noises against the asphalt. "That's German for greetings." He hooked his thumbs into his suspenders proudly.

"What are you wearing?" I asked.

"Lederhosen!" he said, as if he were shocked that I didn't know what the ridiculous homemade shorts he was wearing were called, even though he'd known me for two months and surely had caught on that I never knew what he was talking about. "And a trachten hat." He took off his green hat and bowed with it pressed against his chest. "Pretty cool, huh? So how was school? What did you have for lunch? I made crepes as part of my after-school culinary studies exercise. Chicken cordon bleu flavored." Except he didn't say "blue" like normal people. He said it with an "eh" at the end of it, like, "Blu-eh," which sounded a little like someone throwing up. Which made it sound like he had chicken throw-up for lunch. Which made my Uniquely Gifted lunch of mystery-meat pizza seem much tastier.

"School was fine," I said. I edged toward my house. Chip edged with me. "I have homework, so I should probably go."

"I hardly ever have homework," he said. "Boone Public is way easier than my old school, so I do all my homework

43

in class. Did you know there's a teacher named Mr. Butts? Everyone laughs when you talk about him. I don't get it. Do you get it? He's really nice. What's funny about that?" I shook my head and started to walk away. The kid could tell you what the square root of forty gajillion and eleven was, but he didn't understand a pretty simple middle school joke. "Hey, you seem tense. Should I get my vocabulary socks? I believe today's word of the day is 'amphisbaena.' Many people think a hydra and an amphisbaena are one and the same, but they would be incorrect."

"Who? Who thinks that? Who has even heard of either one of those?" I asked. But when Chip Mason was on a vocabulary roll, it was impossible to sidetrack him.

"But, in fact, a hydra is a serpentlike monster with many heads, and each time you cut one off, two more grow in its place—whereas an amphisbaena is a serpent with one head on each end." He pulled at his suspenders smugly.

"Who have you known who's ever cut the head off a serpent monster, anyway?" I asked.

"Well, Hercules, of course. And then there's Percy Jackson. If you'd like, I can get my mythology socks on and we can delve deeper into the world of the venomous multiheaded beast. It's quite fascinating when you get into the weaponry possibilities of its poisonous blood."

"No, really. I should get going." I started to walk away.

"Okay," he said. "But you still have to show me that water-bending trick, remember?"

"Sure," I said, remembering that, in a fit of weakness when I was trying to just make him stop talking for ten seconds, I had bent water for Chip Mason and had promised to show him how to do it, too. Truthfully, the "trick" was just static electricity, and if Chip thought about it for a minute, he'd probably figure it out on his own, because he was way smarter than any other kid I'd ever known, and probably even smarter than Grandpa Rudy. But I suspected it wasn't as much about the trick as it was about me showing him. Which I would never do. Because all I ever wanted was to get away from Chip Mason. I would be more likely to show him the Stalling Forever trick. I was getting quite masterful at that one. Grandpa Rudy would've been proud.

"Okay, so I'll talk to you tomorrow!" Chip hollered. I turned just in time to see him polka back across the street, yodeling the whole way.

"You really shouldn't have mythology socks," I said to his back.

"I know! I've almost outgrown them. Which means I'll be wearing my British literature socks in no time!" he called without looking back. "I can scarcely wait to dive into *A Tale of Two Cities*. Or walk into, as the case may be."

I supposed if there was one thing I was thankful for, it

was the fact that Chip Mason was going to Boone Public. Otherwise, he'd have been a perfect fit for Pennybaker School.

As if on cue, my chest burst into itchy flames. I ripped off my vest, letting one of the last two intact buttons *plink* onto the driveway and roll away. I wadded the vest under one arm and went inside.

TRICK #5

MAKING SOMETHING OUT OF A CHEESE PUFF NOTHING

"It's all about fooling the eye," I said for the millionth time in the two weeks since I started at Pennybaker School. "It's about making you look over here"—I wiggled the fingers on my left hand to take their eyes away from the grape in my right hand—"to keep you from seeing what's going on over here." I had already deposited the grape into my lap and opened my right hand with flourish.

"Is it true you know how to make an invisibility cloak?" Wesley asked. "Like in Harry Potter?"

"Well, not exactly like in Harry Potter, but kind of, yeah. That's a little more complicated. I'll have you over some time to show you." Although the very thought of Wesley the actor coming anywhere near Chip Mason the costumer made my eye twitch a little. For all I knew, Wesley and Chip Mason could show up in matching Shakespeare socks.

Louis XIV: Bored to death by Shakespeare.

"But, yeah," I continued, making the grape reappear and popping it into my mouth. "I can make stuff disappear by bending light using convex lenses. So it's kind of like an invisibility cloak."

"Whoa," Flea breathed. He had barely touched his lunch and had been sitting, mouth gaping at me, ever since we started talking. Just like every day. Flea thought owning a didgeridoo was normal, but magic was crazy to him.

The truth was I hadn't ever exactly perfected the invisibility cloak. I'd been trying for years, ever since I found the incomplete plans for a "ghosting device" taped to the bottom of Bill's food dish. Grandpa Rudy had been working on an invisibility cloak way ahead of his time, but he must have either given up or died before he could finish it. I'd been trying ever since to perfect it, but while I could make a small object here and there disappear, the idea of shrouding someone into hiddenness was just beyond me.

But it sounded cool, so I went with it.

"Could you make a helicopter disappear?" Flea asked.

I shrugged. "David Copperfield made the Statue of Liberty disappear."

"Can you make my Nationwide History Day project disappear?" Owen asked. Owen was a computer whiz who happened to like to wear a spaghetti strainer, or sometimes an aluminum mixing bowl, on his head because he thought it increased his Internet speed. But he was terrible at history. Once, when Mr. Faboo asked if anyone could name one of Louis XIV's greatest accomplishments, Owen answered, "Invented the corn dog."

Not for nothing, but my answer—"Created neck-torture devices"—was considered no more correct than Owen's corn-dog hypothesis.

"I wish," I said. "I still haven't even decided on a subject yet. I'm definitely not doing the history of the necktie. I was thinking about maybe researching the history of Louis XIV's enemies. Like the ones who really, really hated him and thought up ways to maybe torture him a little or something."

"Nah, that's boring," Owen said. "Mr. Faboo doesn't like boring."

"What's boring about enemies? I bet if Mr. Faboo had enemies, he wouldn't think they were boring at all."

Owen waved his hand. "It's just that kings' enemies are, like, normal history. Mr. Faboo doesn't like normal history."

"Okay. Fine." I thought for a second. "How about the history of Louis Pennybaker?" I asked.

"Been done," Flea said.

Owen nodded, popping a whole cookie into his mouth. He crammed it into one cheek, took a huge swig of milk, and added, "Been done so many times, Mr. Faboo has officially banned it as a topic."

"Louis Pennybaker, born August eleventh, eighteen forty-two," Wesley began in his stage voice.

"Moved to Fair Play, Missouri, in eighteen eighty-six," Flea continued.

Owen swallowed, looking on. "And then to Liberty in eighteen ninety-five, where he—"

"Followed his dream of building a school for kids just like him," Wesley finished.

Flea got up and stood on his chair, one finger in the air. "Kids who were gifted in unique ways. Didgeridoo players."

Wesley stood on his chair. "And thespians, lovers of the theater."

"And computer wizards," Owen said, adjusting the strainer on his head. They all looked at me pointedly, waiting.

"And magicians?" I finally said.

"Grand, old chap," Wesley said, coming down from his chair and clapping me on the back. "Just grand."

"So Louis Pennybaker is out," I said. "Maybe I should do . . ." I searched, then brightened. "The history of the Heirmauser head of horror." I hooked my fingers into claws, rolled my eyes back so only the whites were showing, and growled all monster-like. Which I thought was pretty funny. Erma would have laughed until her guts busted out.

But Wesley, Owen, and Flea, not so much. They all sucked in great gasps of air, then, in unison, turned toward the foyer with their hands over their hearts.

"What? It's just a joke."

"You shouldn't joke about that," Wesley whispered.

"We take the head very, very seriously around here," Flea agreed.

"Mrs. Heirmauser is no laughing matter," Owen added.

"But that thing is super creepy," I said. "It looks like

a zombie. A grandma zombie. Grombie." I rolled my eyes back again and moaned. "Braaains . . . math braaains . . ."

Wesley bent toward me, grabbing my hand and pulling it down to the table. "You could get kicked out for saying something like that."

"Kicked out of life," Flea added. He swept his finger across his throat.

"Sorry. I was just being silly."

"No worries, mate! You're new and all. Forgiven." Wesley was trying out his Australian accent again. Flea and Owen didn't look so sold—they shook their heads at each other somberly, like they weren't sure they could forgive what I'd said as easily as Wesley had. "We just have to get you thinking outside the box." Wesley licked his fingers, which were covered with orange dust. "Hey, I know! You could do cheese puffs!"

"Cheese puffs?"

He nodded, wiggling his half-licked fingers at me. "It's brilliant. I wish I'd thought of it for myself."

"Cheese puffs."

Owen had begun eagerly tapping away on his laptop keyboard. "Yes, yes. Everyone always focuses on boring old leaders who've been done over and over again. What about the creator of the illustrious cheese puff? I mean, where would we be without him?"

"Or her," Flea added.

"Or her," Wesley agreed. "Think about it—there could be a whole unexplored world of cheesy foodstuff innovation. Why let the uninteresting characters in history get all the glory? The inventor of cheese puffs was an American hero!" He licked his thumb clean for emphasis.

"I don't know," I said. It seemed like a risk, pitting the inventor of cheese powder–sprinkled snacks against people who championed animal rights and saved orphans and invented vaccinations or computers or business models. Mom would kill me if I blew my very first Pennybaker School project. I would for sure be going on a Grounded until Christmas Adventure.

Yet, at the same time, Wesley had a point. Cheesy snacks may not have saved the world, but then again neither did Louis Pennybaker. And if I wanted to get all technical about it, cheesy snacks had certainly saved the lunches of millions of kids for generations.

Plus, I didn't have any better ideas.

"Okay," I said. "I'll do it." I slurped my chocolate milk.

"Great!" Wesley said. "Now, with that solved . . ." He pulled the straw out of his milk and held it up. "Has everyone been working on their aim?"

Owen and Flea groaned, but Wesley already knew that I had been working on mine—not because of the upcoming battle in October, but mostly because it was something to do. I'd flung more spitwads at tiny targets than I could even count, including one that actually flipped the switch to turn out the light in Lexiconical Arts when Mrs. Codex stepped out to use the restroom. *"Whoa,"* Wesley had breathed. *"You could put an eye out from a hundred feet!"*

And another that landed square in the head of horror's mouth. Wesley didn't congratulate me on that one; he just grabbed my arm and ran, his face really red and sweaty.

"Okay, Thomas," Wesley said, pushing the still-dripping straw into my hand. "You land one in the nostril of Miss Pancake's potato nose, and I'll officially put you in as team captain. I brought this." He pulled out a straw that was wrapped in brightly colored duct tape. A special team captain straw.

I swiveled in my seat so I could see Miss Pancake, art teacher slash creative free thinker. She was sitting at the kindergarten table, where she had taken everyone's uneaten mashed potatoes and was carefully sculpting them into the shape of a giant nose. The nostrils were about the size of golf balls. Totally doable. But the kindergarten table was across the aisle and two tables away, and Miss Pancake was sitting so that she was facing us, which made the task a bit more challenging.

But I was going to have to be up to the challenge if I wanted to be team captain. And if I wanted that straw.

Oh, I so wanted that straw.

I tore a tiny piece from my napkin, stuck it in my mouth,

and began chewing. Soon I had a soaked napkin-pellet on my tongue. I brought the straw to my mouth, pushed the pellet into it, took a deep breath, and . . .

Someone screamed.

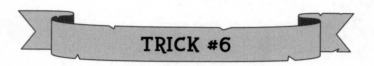

TRICK #6

FLASH! BANG! PANIC!

At first, nobody moved. All eyes turned to me.

"What?" I asked, the straw falling out of my mouth, spit-wad still lodged inside.

"What did you do?" Wesley whispered.

"Nothing. I didn't even blow yet. See?" I turned the straw around to show the slobbery blockage inside.

"He's right," Flea said. "I think the scream came from out there." He was pointing at the lunchroom door, toward the vestibule.

Sure enough, there was another sound—like a low moaning—and all heads in the lunchroom turned.

"No need to panic," Mr. Cheeksbear, the drama teacher, said, standing in the middle of the room with his arms spread out wide. He sounded like Wesley when Wesley was trying on his game-show-host voice. "I'm sure everything is just fi—"

But he didn't get to finish, because another scream pealed through the air, and within seconds, everyone was running.

Not running toward the sound, of course. Sure, a couple of people were running that way, but it appeared to be completely by accident. Instead, people ran every which way, bouncing off each other and the tables, the walls, the milk cooler. Someone knocked over a bench. Another person upended an entire tray of meat loaf. We all stopped to watch the slab of gray hamburger bounce like a rubber ball, right onto the feet of three really mean-looking kids. One picked up a hunk, snarled, and threw it. It landed with a splat on the back of a girl's neck. She squeaked, picked up a handful of Jell-O, calmly walked to another table, and slapped it on top of a boy's head. Next thing we knew, food was flying in every direction.

"Panic! Panic! Panic!" Flea was screaming, running in circles, Owen's metal pot on one foot. "Panic! Panic! Panic!"

"No! Stop that!" Wesley was yelling, though his eyes were very wide, and he was using a plain-old Wesley voice without any acting at all. "You heard the man. There's no need to panic. No need! We should remain calm and rational. Relaxed, even. Let's all breathe in and out slowly together. In through the nose. Out through the mouth. Just like an opening-night warm-up." His face started contorting into frowns and manic-looking stage smiles. "Happy-angry-sad-happy. Happy-angry-sad-happy. Happy-angry-sad-happy."

"Panic! Panic! Panic!"

Owen had pulled open his laptop and was studying the screen intently, having never moved from his seat. "Actually," he said, squinting at me, "I think the best thing to do is to evacuate in an orderly fashion, beginning with the youngest and then going in alphabetical order until we reach grade fi— Would you make him stop doing that?"

"Panic! Panic! Panic!" Flea had somehow stepped in the potato nose and was leaving mushy white splotches everywhere.

I climbed up on top of the table, unsure how I was going to get everyone's attention. Then it dawned on me. I had two spark ejectors, locked and loaded with flash paper and batteries, in my pocket. As magicians tend to have.

I pulled them out, took a deep breath, and yelled, "Everyone stop!" I held my arms out with a flourish, threw my head back, and . . . showstopper.

Or not.

Nothing happened, other than a weak buzzing sound and a little plop of light that might just as easily have been a dying firefly.

Nobody noticed. Not even Owen, whose slice of rubber

meat loaf was currently resting under the toe of my penny loafer.

"I've got nothing," I said, but only I was listening. I climbed off the bench and sat down. Someone had flung a half-eaten cheese puff in my direction. It skittered across the table and came to a stop right in front of me. I picked it up and munched on it. From what I could tell, this school's most unique gift was being annoying.

But just as I swallowed my cheese puff, Milly and Hilly, two ponytailed fourth graders, appeared in the lunchroom doorway.

"Terrible happening, everyone!" Hilly said. The lunchroom went instantly quiet.

"Heirmauser's elegant art donation . . . happened about second . . . before everyone's eyes, nearly," Milly said, her voice hitching on the last word.

"Swiped, taken, or lifted even now!" Hilly screeched.

There was a long pause while everyone seemed to be calculating in their heads. And then there was a collective gasp and a mass exodus toward the vestibule.

"What happened?" I asked.

"The horror!" Wesley responded in a horror-movie voice, whisking past me.

"What's going on?"

Flea clunked by in his pot-boot, not even acknowledging that he heard me speak.

Owen got up and started that way as well. I grabbed his arm. "Can you please tell me what's happening?"

"Didn't you hear Hilly and Milly?"

"Yeah, but they made no sense."

He rolled his eyes. "They speak in acrostic. It's their gift."

I shook my head, still not understanding.

"You don't know what an acrostic is?" He looked impatient. "It's a poem style where the first letter of every word spells out a new word. 'Terrible Happening, Everyone.' T-H-E. 'Heirmauser's Elegant Art Donation.' H-E-A-D. 'Happened About Second.' H-A-S. 'Before Everyone's Eyes, Nearly.' B-E-E-N. 'Swiped, Taken, Or Lifted Even Now.' S-T-O-L-E-N." We stared at each other for a moment, then he grasped my shoulders and shook me. "Don't you get it, man? During second period, someone stole Helen Heirmauser's head!"

Owen looked horrified at having said the actual words aloud. He pressed one hand over his mouth and raced toward the vestibule, leaving his prized laptop on the table where he'd been sitting.

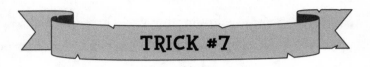

TRICK #7

VANISHED!

Sure enough, the head was gone. In its place on top of the pedestal was a round spot of darker paint that had been shielded from sunlight beneath the head. Miss Munch was crumpled to the floor next to the pedestal, holding a tissue in one fist.

"It's gone," she whimpered over and over again. "It's gone."

Several students in various states of distress and sadness gathered around her. Some of the girls were draped over the shoulders of their friends as if they might faint at any moment.

"Who would do such a thing?" Owen whispered, gaping in awe at the empty pedestal. "Who would want to steal the head?" He tapped some calculations into his watch and still came up with nothing.

"Exactly what I was thinking," I said, only I don't think I meant it in the same way that he did.

"Maybe one of the custodians took it for polishing," Principal Rooster said, shoving his way through the crowd. I hadn't really seen the principal of Pennybaker School much yet. I had only heard his voice over the intercom, reciting the Pledge of Allegiance and the Pennybaker School pledge:

UNIQUELY GIFTED STUDENTS ARE WE.
WE HAVE A TALENT, OR MAYBE THREE.
LOYAL TO OUR SCHOOL WE WILL ALWAYS BE.
WITH PRIDE, WORK, AND HONESTY
BEFITTING OUR FOUNDER, WHOSE NAME WAS LOU-EE.

Principal Rooster reminded me a little bit of Grandpa Rudy. He was kind of short and squat, with soft-looking cheeks and a ring of gray fringy hair. The lights reflected off the top of his head and his glasses, making him look like a walking lightbulb. He had the kind of mouth that always looked like it was smiling, and it was hard to imagine him bringing down the hammer on a bad kid.

Maybe they didn't have bad kids at Pennybaker School. Maybe Principal Rooster's job was a really long Nothing to Do Adventure.

"Yes, yes, it's being cleaned," he said, shoving his hands into his suit pockets and rocking back on his heels, as if he'd solved a major crime. "It has been a while since her forehead was buffed. I'm sure of it now. Miss Munch, gather the custodians, please. We'll get to the bottom of this."

Miss Munch looked up miserably from where she sat on the floor. Her nose was red and runny. "Byron's out today."

"Well, gather the others, then," Principal Rooster said. "We'll have this whole matter straightened out in no time." He helped Miss Munch off the floor, patted her shoulder a few times, then clapped twice. "Now, the bell should be ringing at any moment. Everyone go ahead and move on to your next class."

I started to go and almost plowed right into the kid in front of me. Like everyone else, he didn't move a muscle. They all just kind of stood there, looking at each other with their mouths open. A slice of cheese fell off someone's shoulder and landed with a splat on the floor.

"Go on," Principal Rooster commanded, waving his hands around like he was shooing bugs away. "To class."

"We can't," a kid on the other side of the room piped up. There were murmurs of agreement. Heads began nodding.

"With all due respect, sir," a very serious-looking eighth grader said, "we don't think it's right for us to just go on learning when Mrs. Heirmauser's head is out there somewhere."

"With a stranger," a girl with jagged bangs added.

"Or lost," a kindergartner chimed in. "All alone and lonely."

Now the crowd was getting restless.

"How can we be expected to pay attention in class when Mrs. Heirmauser isn't here?" Patrice Pillow asked through the curtain of jet black hair that fell over her entire face, only the bump of a nose sticking through. "What if it was a madman who took it, and he's going to use it to dispatch his next victim?" She ground one fist violently into the palm of her other hand. "Or a ghost made off with it and is going to drop it on the head of an unsuspecting student. Right when they don't suspect it. When they suspect nothing." She whipped a notebook out of her back pocket and began writing. Patrice Pillow was in my Lexiconical Arts class. She had been writing a horror novel since she was three.

I decided to have a go at it. I cleared my throat. "Oh, or what if it was beamed up into outer space by head-stealing aliens, and we're all next? And then there's a creepy voice that comes out of an old barn, because there are always old barns in these types of situations, right, and, wait—no, it's a baby. A baby crying in an old barn, and maybe some, like, creepy whispering or something. No, no. Little kids laughing. Yeah, little kids laughing. And then when you go in and open the door—which is, of course, super creaky and, like, covered with spiders and some gross slime and stuff—you follow the noise to a back corner, dig under some old straw, and there it is. The Heirmauser Head of Horror." I threw my head back and let out an evil laugh without thinking.

Everyone stared. It got very quiet. I felt my face flood over with sweat. "I thought we were plotting her novel," I said. "Never mind."

"This isn't a joke, whoever you are," a boy carrying a net over his shoulder said. He had a wedge of grease on his shirt in the exact shape of a slice of pizza. He must have been hit by one during the mayhem.

"Sorry," I mumbled, ducking behind Wesley, who looked like he wanted to do anything other than protect me.

"You pick now to become a thespian?" he whispered.

"I got carried away," I whispered back. "I'm sorry."

Miss Munch came back into the vestibule with two custodians—the ones I knew only as Mr. Crumbs and Zelda the Mop—trailing behind her. Mr. Crumbs took one look at the empty pedestal and let out a small screech. He swayed, and Zelda the Mop caught him. Principal Rooster seemed shaken. He cleared his throat, pulled his hands out of his pockets, and crossed his arms, rolling back on his heels again as he tried to recuperate.

"Excellent. John, Rose, I'm sure you'll be able to solve this whole mystery."

"Who are John and Rose?" Flea whispered.

"Heck if I know," Wesley whispered back. "I guess they must be Crumbs and Mop."

This seemed to unsettle Flea, as if he really thought that maybe Mr. Crumbs and Zelda the Mop were born with those names. Like Crumbs's mom took one look at her little baby and said, *"My, that looks like a Mr. Crumbs to me."* Although . . . if I squinted and turned my head just right, I could kind of see that happening.

"I . . . I don't know what you mean," Mr. Crumbs said nervously. Behind him, Zelda the Mop shook her head.

"You didn't remove the bust?" Principal Rooster said, waving toward the pedestal impatiently. "You aren't cleaning it?" Mr. Crumbs swooned again and sagged into Mop's arms.

"We've been in the second-grade hallway all morning," she said. "Stomach bug," she whispered, and everyone in the crowd grimaced and scooted away from the second graders.

"So . . . so you don't know where it is," Principal Rooster said. He had stopped rocking back on his heels. A bead of sweat rolled over the top of his head and down into his ear. Seeing it made my ear tickle, but I was afraid to scratch it. The entire crowd seemed to be holding its breath, and even the smallest move might make the school pop like a balloon.

"No, sir," Mop said. Mr. Crumbs shook his head weakly as she said it.

"Well, that confirms it," Miss Munch declared, her eyes wide and roving. "Mrs. Heirmauser's head has been stolen."

Mayhem took over again.

There was yelling and raising of fists, and some third-grade girls were sobbing loudly.

66

Everyone started milling about and bumping into each other. There were angry shouts of *"Watch it!"* and *"Ouch, that was my foot!"* and even one *"Your pencil is in my ear!"* Principal Rooster kept patting the air, his mouth held in shushing formation, the actual shushing unheard through the chaos. Finally, a boy I recognized from my Active Numbering class scrambled up the stairs and called down.

"Oy!"

Instant silence. We all looked up. He stood on the stair rail, balanced perfectly. I guessed his unique

gift was something death-defying that Grandma Jo could really appreciate.

"Let's stop yelling," he said, once he had everyone's attention. "All of us need to calm down."

"Yes, yes, thank you, Stephen," Principal Rooster said. "Now, if you will all go back to cl—"

"We'll never find the statue if we keep panicking!" Stephen hollered, and the crowd cheered.

"No, no," Principal Rooster said, patting the air again. "We need to get back to studyin—"

"Leave no corner unexamined! No desk unturned! We. Will. Find. That. Head!" Stephen pumped his fist into the sky, and now the crowd had momentum. The random milling and bumping turned into frenzied milling and bumping with a purpose as kids went every which way, leaving a flustered Principal Rooster with puffed-out cheeks and Miss Munch next to the pedestal, fanning Crumbs's face.

I just stood there and watched. This was hands-down the craziest thing I'd ever seen, and I once saw Grandma Jo climb all the way to the top of the Boone County water tower in her Sunday dress.

I was just about to go back into the cafeteria to see if any of my lunch could be salvaged when I noticed one kid moving differently from everyone else. It was a sixth grader. He was in my Claymaking class. I thought his name was Reap.

Reap was pale, with messy brown hair and freckles you could see from across the room.

He was coming out of the cafeteria, his eyes shifting this way and that, his body hunkered over and his shoulders stooped. His hands clutched the bottom of his vest, which was rounded by something big hidden underneath.

Wesley wandered by, perfecting the pensive chin-scratch of an old-fashioned movie detective. I grabbed his sleeve. "Hey, you see that?" I pointed at Reap.

Reap hurried across the foyer and out the front door. Wesley's eyes narrowed, his lips pooched together. He rubbed his chin between his finger and thumb so hard I was pretty sure he was going to leave a red spot there.

"He was totally hiding something under his vest," I said. "Something big."

"Hmmm," Wesley said. "Very curious." I was pretty sure he was trying on a Sherlock Holmes voice.

I grabbed his sleeve again. "Let's follow him. I'll bet he has the head on him right now and is getting ready to hide it."

"Yes, yes," Wesley said.

But we got only two steps toward the door before someone yelled, "To the garden!"

"The garden!" the crowd cheered, and the entire school surged in the exact opposite direction of where we were trying to go.

"Where's the garden?" I asked Wesley, trying to stand my ground, which was hard to do with everyone in the school smashing into me.

"Back door," Wesley cried, moving along with the crowd.

Before I could even fight it, I was swept away by the sea of kids, too. "To the garden," I said weakly, casting one last glance toward the front door, where Reap had gotten away.

TRICK #8

ABRACADABRA AND ENTEMWHATEVERGY

Chip Mason was lying flat on his back in the middle of his front yard, counting loudly, when I got home.

"I just can't even imagine who would steal something like that," Mom said, climbing out of the car. "And in the middle of the day, too. What is this world coming to that people just make off with other people's heads in the middle of lunch and force the principal to send everyone home?"

"Mm-hmm," I said, because I really didn't care who'd made off with Mrs. Heirmauser's head. I was actually kind of glad about it, because I got half the day off. Not to mention, as long as it stayed missing, I wouldn't have to stop to pay my respects every time I passed through the vestibule. My sore knees could use a rest.

Plus, I had the team captain straw. Wesley was too

distraught to care when I asked if I had the job. He just nodded and waved.

"This is very disturbing. I don't suppose you saw anything? Heard anything? Noticed someone different lurking around?"

"Seven hundred forty-two," Chip Mason intoned from his yard. Speaking of someone different.

"Nope."

"Well," Mom huffed, shouldering her purse. "I suppose heads are going to roll over this." Then, realizing what she said, she blushed bright red and tightened her purse strap even higher. "I mean, someone's in for a load of trouble. As they should be. From what I've heard, stealing Helen Heirmauser's head is like stealing the . . . the . . . national anthem!"

"How can you steal the national—?" I began, but was cut off when the garage door rumbled to life.

"Did someone say trouble?" Grandma Jo asked. She was wearing a glittery hot-pink helmet and knee pads with stars and rainbows on them, and had a skateboard tucked under her arm. Mom gasped.

"Look at it this way, Mom," I said, trying to take her attention away from Grandma Jo. "At least I'm not the one in trouble this time. I had nothing to do with that thing. The less I have to do with it, the better, as far as I'm concerned."

"Seven hundred forty-three!"

"No, but your Grandma Jo is looking for trouble, I can see," Mom said, yanking her purse strap up over her shoulder so tightly that her purse was basically buried in her armpit. I reminded myself not to ask Mom for gum for a while, or at least until Erma had chewed all the armpit gum. "And just where do you think you're going, Mother?" she called, stomping toward the garage.

"Those fellas at the skate park invited me to join them," Grandma Jo said. "They're gonna teach me how to Gingersnap."

I didn't know what a Gingersnap was, but I was pretty sure that no matter what it was, there was no way in the world Mom was going to let Grandma Jo have a Gingersnap Adventure with the fellas at the skate park.

"You're going nowhere," Mom said, hands on her hips. Even for all that cinching up, her purse still slid down her arm and thunked at her wrist.

"Says you," Grandma Jo said, placing her hands on her hips, too, the skateboard staying snug against her side. "Barf is expecting me, and I don't want to let him down."

Mom's eyes bugged out of her head. "You're going to skateboard with someone named Barf? Are you even hearing yourself right now?"

"Seven hundred forty-four!"

"Oh, now, Barf is a perfectly nice boy. It's Sludge you

have to worry about. But I'm pretty sure Sludge has a broken leg right now, so she shouldn't be too hard to handle today."

"Sludge . . . ? *She . . . ?* Broken . . . ?"

As much as I liked to avoid Chip Mason whenever I possibly could, and as much as I was interested in hearing about the Saga of Barf and Sludge and whoever else would be at the skate park with Grandma Jo, I knew that when Mom got to the one-word-sentence portion of an argument, things were about to get really scary really fast. Scarier than screaming-haunted-head scary.

Plus, I was a little curious about what he was counting.

I walked across the street.

"Seven hundred forty-five!" Chip sat up, high-fived himself, and flopped back down. "Hey, Thomas," he said, though his eyes never shifted to look at me at all.

I glanced upward, trying to figure out what he was looking at. I saw nothing but sky. "What are you doing?"

"Counting."

I rolled my eyes. "I know that. What are you counting?"

He patted the ground next to him very subtly. "Shhh. Lie flat and pretend you don't exist. They can sense awareness. It's a survival thing."

This was not the weirdest thing Chip Mason had ever said to me, but it came pretty close to ranking in the top five.

Current Top Five Weirdest Things Chip Mason Has Said to Me with No Explanation, Ranked in Order from Off-Putting to Outright Disturbing

5) "If a leopard frog is ever staring at you really hard and his eyes start to swallow, you should run."

4) "It would be impossible for you to be the first person to pee on the moon."

3) "My tongue print looks like the *Portrait of Eugène Boch*. See?"

2) "Did you know you could make a piano out of live cats?"

1) "When eating casu marzu, you should always make sure to shield your eyes so the maggots don't jump into them."

Still, I lowered myself to the ground and lay flat on my back, just like he said to do. Which probably says more about me than it does about Chip Mason.

"Seven hundred forty-six," he said. "But it'll probably be a few minutes before I get to seven hundred forty-seven. Since you disturbed the atmosphere and all."

"Seven hundred forty-seven what?" I asked, searching the sky, thinking maybe he was counting clouds or birds or leaves on a tree or something.

"Bugs," he said simply. "I'm taking a science enrichment day off from school today. Seven hundred forty-six bugs have landed on me. Every nerve in my body is in tune with the atmosphere. I feel every tiny insect foot that traverses my epidermis. I don't even have to look to know that there's a ladybug—that's Coccinellidae—on my ankle, and a fly—Diptera, of course—on my forehead. Seven hundred forty-seven and seven hundred forty-eight, by the way." He scratched his forehead, and sure enough a fly took to the air. "It was really hopping out here right around dawn, but I seem to have gotten another good run just over the past forty-five minutes or so. Maybe a bug convention let out nearby." He giggled. "I'm being ridiculous, of course. Bugs tend to hold their conventions during the winter."

"You got a day off from school and you were out here counting bugs at dawn?"

"Can you think of a better time?"

Yes. How about never? I wanted to say, but I didn't really have the energy to bust Chip Mason's chops right now, especially given that I was lying in the yard with him, and, yes, I had started to mentally keep tally of the five—wait, six—flies that had briefly landed on me since I'd gotten down here. Why were there so many flies?

I sniffed the air and wrinkled my nose. "Do you smell something?"

"Oh, it's probably my entomology socks," he said, reaching down and pulling off a brown sock.

"Entomology socks?"

"The study of insects," he said. He dangled the sock over my face, and the stench intensified by nine thousand. "I soaked them in rotting fruit and old hamburger for thirteen days," he said proudly. "I could attract some really exciting Insecta with these. If I stayed out here long enough, I would become a ripe breeding ground for maggots. Pretty amazing, when you think about it, that maggots could writhe around inside my socks, feeding off the garbage enzymes, until they molted into pupae."

I batted the putrid sock away, gagging. "Are you crazy? That thing reeks. How could you put that on your body? It could kill a horse."

Louis XIV: Devoured from the feet up by rancid entemwhatevergy socks. Tongue permanently tied from saying entemwhatevergy.

"I doubt it could actually kill a horse, but it could definitely feed an infantile horse*fly*," Chip said, grinning, taking the sock back and draping it over one knee. Instantly, three flies gathered on it. "Seven hundred fifty-one, by the way."

Across the street, Mom's argument with Grandma Jo escalated.

"So your grandma is a skateboarder, huh?" Chip asked. "I wish Grandpa Huck could still do stuff like that."

"Your grandpa would have skateboarded?" Translation: The man who invented mean did things that made people smile?

"Never," Chip said. "At least I don't think so. I didn't really spend a whole lot of time with him before he got sick. In a way, his getting sick has been a good thing for our family. Which sounds like a terrible thing to say. But I'm learning a lot about him. Did you know he went to the school you're going to?"

"Ugh, don't remind me that I go there."

Chip Mason shrugged. "Can't be worse than Boone Public. This might surprise you, but I'm not very popular there. I'm having trouble securing friendships, even though I wore my sociology socks for an entire month straight."

"From the smell of things, that might be why you can't make any friends."

He sat up, his entomology sock sliding off his knee and tumbling into the grass, taking a bevy of flies with it. He pulled off the other sock and wiggled his bare toes, which were somehow grosser than his socked toes were. I could imagine some of the popular guys at Boone Public—Brandon, Gavin, and Paris—making puke noises while listening to Chip talk about bugs and rotted stuff. I could imagine them laughing at him when he said words like "entomology" or talked about his astrophysics socks. I could totally hear them telling Chip to take a hike and see them making him sit at the Unfortunate Bologna Incident lunch table. A part of me hoped this was all in my imagination, because even though I avoided Chip whenever possible and thought he was pretty much the weirdest person in the world, it still made me sad to think about people treating him that way.

"Give it time. You'll make friends."

"Nah, I don't think so. But that's okay. I have other friends. I have Mom and Grandpa Huck. And you. Hey, come to think of it, Thomas," he said, "you're the best friend I ever had."

I sat up, too. No. No, no, no. I did not want to be Chip Mason's best friend. Quickly, I tried to conjure up an image of my real best friend, Dustin, who'd gone to Boone Public Elementary with me. We had ridden our bikes together for miles. We'd eaten more Pizza Rolls than anyone could even count. We'd wrestled and swapped homework and even held hands with girls on the same skating party night in fifth grade. Dustin was my best friend.

My best friend, whom I hadn't heard from even one time since I started going to Pennybaker School.

My best friend who walked right past me at the ice cream shop last Saturday with Duncan Flannery, of all people, and didn't even say hi.

My best friend who, let's face it, wasn't my best friend anymore.

But hey, you have Wesley, I tried to tell myself. *You have Flea and Owen and even spine-chilling Patrice Pillow. You*

have all the (oddball) unique (kooky) gifted (freaky) students at
Pennybaker School. You may not exactly fit in right now, but
you're working on it, and before you know it, you will spitwad
your way to best friendom with . . . with . . .

I sighed. *With nobody.*

"Seven hundred sixty-two," Chip murmured next to me, inspecting the collection of bugs on his socks. A fly landed on his finger. "Sorry, little buddy. You'll have to lay your larvae somewhere else. Mom will kill me if I let you pupate on my feet."

But especially not with Chip Mason.

I stood, grateful that the elevation took me out of the rancid sock cloud. "I've gotta go," I said. "I think maybe Mom needs some help." Grandma Jo had mounted her skateboard and was currently careening down the driveway with Mom running behind her, shouting things about broken hips and hospital bills and spring chickens. From the look of things, she wasn't going to catch Grandma Jo anytime soon.

We watched as Mom stopped at the end of the driveway and raced back to her purse, which she'd dropped by the garage door, then grabbed her car keys and ran to the car, yelling, "I will see you and Barf and Booger and Zit and whoever else is going to teach you to Gingersnap at the skate park! You'll see, Mother! You! Will! See!" She got in and zoomed to about a foot behind Grandma Jo and then slow-speed chased her around the corner.

"Oh, good! You're free!" Chip said, standing and brushing off the back of his shorts.

"No, I'm pretty sure I need to . . . do something . . . for when she comes back. Dinner, probably."

"But it's only twelve thirty."

"Complicated dinner. And I'm not a very good cook. Plus, I should probably call Dad."

"Perhaps you'd like to come inside for a serous ichor of citric acid, sucrose, and Adam's ale?"

As usual, I had no idea what he was talking about, but, given that he was holding a pair of the stinkiest socks ever in existence, I figured there was a good chance I didn't want a "serious ick" of anything he had to offer.

Seeing the look of confusion on my face, he grinned.

"That's a liquid mixture of lemon, sugar, and water." I still wasn't getting it. "Lemonade!" he clarified. "Perhaps you would like to come inside for some lemonade? Or I can bring it out here."

"Oh, uh . . . no thanks. I need to take off my uniform." Although I'd learned how to tie my tie sort of properly by now, I was beginning to suspect that it would never stop being scratchy and miserable.

"Okay, but maybe after you're done you can come back out and show me a new trick?"

"I don't have any new tricks." *If I did, I would make you disappear*, I thought. I had edged all the way to the street, but Chip Mason followed me, matching me one tiny step at a time, so that it seemed like neither of us had ever moved at all.

"You could show me an old one, then. I don't mind."

"I'm sort of out of magic," I said.

He flung his head back and laughed. I got to see all of his teeth. "Out of magic! Whoo-hoo-hoo! Ah-ha-ha!" He bent forward and slapped his knee a few times, a cloud of bugs lifting off the socks in his hand and landing again. He wiped his eyes with one. I held back a gag. "You're a real cutup, Thomas Fallgrout. Out of magic. As if that's possible."

I had no idea what I'd said that was so funny. The truth was, since going to Pennybaker School, I hadn't done as much magic as I used to. Which was ironic, given that I was at Pennybaker *because* of my magic. We were all encouraged to use our special and unique gifts in our classwork, but that was easier for someone like Owen, whose computer skills actually helped his classwork, than it was for someone like me. What was I going to do? Saw my assignments in half? Suddenly I had an urge to boil water in a paper bag or turn blue water clear.

I pulled a deck of cards out of my pocket.

"Okay. Here, Chip," I said. "Pick a card, but don't tell me what it is . . ."

TRICK #9

PRODUCING A SMUGGLER OUT OF THIN AIR

I still had a lot of day left, and I was bored. After I taught Chip a few card tricks, he was so wrapped up in perfecting them that he completely forgot I was there. Erma got home from school and immediately began watching TV. And Mom and Grandma Jo had never come home.

I plopped on my bed and bounced a tennis ball off the ceiling, trying to distract myself from the troubling realization that I was so bored I would rather have been at school. It's unfair the way the brain works against you sometimes.

I wondered what tomorrow would be like. Surely everyone would have calmed down by then. Maybe the statue would have even been returned. All a big misunderstanding.

A big misunderstanding that Reap had something to do with. That, I was sure of.

I rolled off my bed and went downstairs.

"Erma, where's the laptop?"

"Shhh!" she hissed. "This is a good part."

"I just want to find the laptop."

"So open your eyes." She still had never looked away from the TV. I was starting to wonder if her eyes were magnetically fused to it.

"Where did you last put it?"

"I didn't. Hush."

"You were the last one to use it, Erma."

Finally she turned around, her face an angry splot. "If you don't be quiet, I'm telling Mom that you were bouncing a ball off your ceiling again." I picked up the remote and just stared at her, pointing it toward the TV, until she rolled her eyes. "Fine. I used it in the kitchen."

I tossed the remote to her. "Was that so hard?"

"Shhh!"

Sisters.

I found the laptop and opened it, pulling up the Pennybaker homework chat site—a webpage that was designed for students to help each other finish projects. There was always someone on it, and usually that someone was Wesley— the most extroverted person who ever attended Pennybaker School.

Sure enough, he was logged in, so I messaged him.

TFallgrout: Hey

StageStar: Hey Thomas, what's up?

TFallgrout: I was thinking about the head of horror just now

StageStar: . . .

TFallgrout: Okay, okay, I mean the statue

StageStar: What about it?

TFallgrout: Reap

StageStar: ???

TFallgrout: I think he had it under his vest. He looked really suspeesh sushipsh suspecc

StageStar: Suspicious?

TFallgrout: Yeah that. He definitely didn't want to get caught carrying whatever he was carrying. THE ZOMBIE HEAD.

StageStar: I am making a stellar stop-that face at you right now.

TFallgrout: Ok ok. Let's confront him

StageStar: Who?

TFallgrout: REAP!!!!!!!

StageStar: That's a jolly idea, ol' boy. I say yea and a pip pip.

(Wesley was convinced that people could hear his accents online.)

TFallgrout: So tomorrow? We can follow him out of
  Claymaking and wait until we get him alone.
StageStar: And den smash bang crash we'll have da
  moichendise back, see?

(Okay, so maybe he was right about the accent thing
sometimes.)

TFallgrout: Everyone will be happy
StageStar: We will be heroes!
TFallgrout: See you tomorrow before school for you
  know what practice?
StageStar: Bright and early!

I signed off and shut the laptop, feeling much less bored
now that I had a plan to think about. We would follow Reap.
We would get him alone. We would make him confess.
  And we would get the statue back.

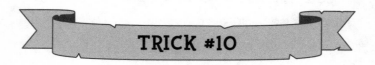

TRICK #10

VANISH ALL THE THINGS!

Mom and Grandma Jo were trying to set grouchiness records the next morning. Turned out Grandma Jo had shaken Mom on the way to the skate park by grabbing on to the bumper of a passing pickup truck, and by the time Mom found which skate park she was at, Barf and someone named Shredding Fred were teaching her how to do a Salad Grind. Mom stepped in and tweaked Shredding Fred's nose, refusing to let go until Grandma Jo was in the car. The skateboarders gave Mom a nickname that Mom refused to repeat while Erma and I were in the room, and Grandma Jo gave Mom an even worse nickname than that. They'd been snapping at each other all morning.

"Would you like some scrambled eggs, Mother?" Mom asked when Grandma Jo came into the room.

"I probably shouldn't. I might burn my tongue or poke my lip with the fork."

"Oh, Mother, don't be like that. Here, have some coffee. You'll feel better."

"Are you sure it's safe for me to do that? Maybe you should call my babysitter. Oh, wait. You *are* my babysitter."

"I am not your babysitter!"

"Well, you're sure acting like one!"

"Only because if I didn't, who knows what sort of antics you'd get into?"

On and on they went, Erma and I pretending we weren't there, just in case Mom or Grandma Jo should decide we needed to take a side. Or worse, in case Mom or Grandma Jo got irritated enough to make one of us clean up the breakfast dishes.

When Dad came through to grab a cup of coffee on the way out, I sprang up from the table.

"Hey, Dad? Can you give me a ride today? I need to get there early."

"Of course, buddy," Dad said, unplugging his phone from its charger and slipping it into his pocket. "Be ready to leave in five minutes."

"Me, too," Erma said, jumping up next to me. Ordinarily I would have been irritated that she was tagging along and would tell her to buzz off and stop being such a pest. But as

Grandma Jo pointed to the paper towel roll and asked Mom, "Permission to tear off a towel, sir? It has sharp corners and I might put an eye out," I understood why Erma wanted to go to school early today, too.

Chip Mason was outside as we pulled away, school backpack on, staring through a telescope into a knothole in the big tree in his front yard instead of standing with the rest of the kids at the bus stop. There was no way he was seeing anything but infinite blackness. Or at least that was what a normal person would have seen. Who knew what Chip Mason would see? He probably had his miniature civilization socks on and was looking into an entire society.

Erma waved manically at him, even though he didn't see her. Erma was just weird enough to like Chip Mason without being forced to.

"It's probably a good thing you're going to school early today," Dad said as he pulled onto the highway. "Mom and Grandma Jo are in a real pickle of a mood this morning."

"You should have stayed home with them, Thomas picklepuss," Erma said from the backseat. I looked in the side mirror and saw her cross her eyes at me. I ignored her.

"They'll get over it," Dad said. "They're just having growing pains."

"I thought growing pains were for teenagers," I said. "And were actual pains."

Dad thought about it. "Sometimes growing pains are

just about figuring out a new way to do things. Mom and Grandma Jo are trying to figure out how to do . . . this."

Mom and Grandma Jo were having a Growing Pain Adventure. From the look of things, it wasn't any better than actual pains.

"So, speaking of growing pains, how are things going with your new school? I hope that going in early doesn't mean you're having troubles that I need to know about."

"No, it's just a . . . meeting," I said.

"Oh, a club?" Dad brightened, glancing at me excitedly before reaching for his coffee.

I shrugged. "Sure, I guess you could say that."

"What kind? Running club? Debate? Ooh, did you start a magic club?"

I thought about it. The spitwad war was like magic in a lot of ways. We were meeting in secret, working hard on our skills by practicing them over and over again, and if we were to get caught and interrogated by Nurse Nothing That Involves Spit Is Fun, we would never tell how it was done.

"Yeah. Kind of," I said. "It's a secret sort of club."

"Mom says it isn't nice to keep secrets," Erma said from the backseat.

"Can it, Erma," I said. "It's not a secret from Mom, so it doesn't count."

"Sounds like a fun club," Dad said, pulling up the long drive to Pennybaker School. All our heads angled over to the right, just like they always did when we approached the crooked school. "Just make sure you're letting everyone be a part."

"Oh, trust me, everyone is a part," I said. Word was most of the school was now involved somehow. Walk down the hall without protective headgear and you ran the risk of showing up to class looking spackled.

"Huh. Seems pretty quiet," Dad said, coming to a stop in front of the building. Mr. Crumbs was outside, listlessly sweeping the steps, but there was nobody else around.

"They're probably meeting in the cafeteria," I said. But I was unsure. Wesley said we would have our meetings on the steps, and Wesley never missed an opportunity to practice a monologue on an elevated surface. I didn't want to take the chance that Dad might take me back home to Mom and Grandma Jo's fight or Chip Mason's . . . whatever it was he was doing with that telescope, so I opened the door and shouldered my backpack. "See ya!"

"Wouldn't wanna be ya," Erma said, but I shut the door without paying her any attention.

"Have a good day, pal," Dad said through his open window. "See you at dinner!"

Dad pulled away, and it was just me and the *shhh-shhh* of Mr. Crumbs's broom.

"Um, excuse me?" I asked hesitantly. I'd never actually talked to Crumbs before, and after seeing him the other day, I was half afraid he'd pass out on me if I startled him. "Hello?"

His eyes flicked up toward me and he grunted. I guessed that was his way of asking what he could help me with.

I cleared my throat. "Have you seen anybody else? Other kids, I mean? My friend Wesley, maybe? The kid who always has an encore at lunch?"

Crumbs never stopped moving, never stopped sweeping. Although I don't know that I would actually call it sweeping, as half the time the broom just barely grazed the ground. The same dead ivy leaf swirled in lazy circles each time he moved past it. "I haven't seen anybody, kid," he said. "Maybe you should check inside."

I hurried away before he started getting swoony, and pulled open the big, heavy doors. They had a creak. Not like a normal creak, but one of those metal-on-metal creaks that make you think about things popping out of graves and stuff.

I'd never noticed that creak before. How had I never noticed that creak before?

The answer occurred to me the minute I walked into the vestibule.

The empty, completely silent vestibule.

Never before had I realized how noisy the foyer at Pennybaker School always was. It wasn't just the entrance to the school; it was the gathering place for the students. It was where romances started and ended, where jokes were told, assignments finished, disagreements ironed out, stories reenacted. It was where everyone felt the most . . . alive.

Right next to the dead head. Made no sense to me.

I realized, after sensing some movement, that there was somebody in the vestibule with me after all. A custodian—one I'd never seen before—was standing behind the now-empty pedestal. I'd heard of another custodian at Pennybaker. His name was Byron. He hung out in the basement, mostly, and was a little strange. But nobody would ever tell me exactly how he was strange. I had lots of theories.

Theory #1: Byron the Rat King, who spent his time in the basement lording over his kingdom of furry, pink-eyed residents. He taught them sign language and potty-trained them and fed them students' tears for dinner.

Theory #2: Byron the Vampire, who couldn't come out of the basement during daylight hours for obvious reasons. Of course, now that I'd seen him standing in a beam of sunlight behind the pedestal first thing in the morning, it was clear that the vampire theory had some holes in it.

Theory #3: Byron the Student, who hadn't come out of the basement since he failed his seventh-grade science test in 1982 and still tells his parents he "just hasn't graduated yet."

Theory #4: Byron the Alligator-Human Hybrid. I hadn't really fleshed this one out yet, because every time I thought about it, I got lost in the awesomeness of it all and started thinking up theme songs.

But at the moment, he was just Byron, the custodian with a huge shrub of jet-black hair and a pointed nose that dipped so low it nearly rested on his chin. In one hand, he held a dirty blue rag, stained with gray spots and limp with cleaner. He was frozen, rooted to his spot, as he stared at me and I stared at him.

I was just getting ready to ask him if he'd seen Wesley or anyone else carrying a bundle of straws and paper when he quickly swished the rag over the top of the pedestal and down each side, and then darted off through the back hallway that led to the basement stairs.

I stood for a moment, alone in the silent, empty vestibule, wondering what I'd just seen. "Ohhh-kay," I said aloud, and then said to myself what I'd said about a billion times since starting here, "That was definitely unique."

I passed through the vestibule, my penny loafers clicking especially penny-loaferly against the tile floor, and headed for the cafeteria. There was nobody there, and it was dead quiet except for maybe some faint rodenty scurrying, which I pretended not to notice, because who wants to notice rodents in the same place where your grilled cheese and tomato soup are cooked? I wound through the first floor hallway to the theater, thinking maybe Wesley had been struck with a sudden need to Hamlet (which, yes, he used as a verb, and which tended to happen more often than you would think). But the theater was dark, Mr. Cheeksbear sitting silently in the front row, watching a stage full of nothing. There was nobody in the greenhouse, nobody in any of the restrooms, and only Miss Munch, still clutching a crinkled tissue in one hand, in the office.

It was really starting to freak me out.

I pushed through a side door to the small, rusted playground that was used for the elementary kids.

There, I finally found Wesley, Flea, Owen, and two other boys I recognized from our Facts After the Fact class. They were sitting in a loose circle, Wesley's back propped against the brick wall, his hands draped between his knees.

"Oh. Hey, Thomas," Wesley said. Only he said it in a normal Wesley voice. No British accent. No Western twang. No mobster act or cartoon voice or reenactment from a movie. He didn't have a scarf tied around his neck or his hair slicked back or any leftover stage makeup on. It was sort of startling to see him that way.

"Hey," I said, letting the door shut behind me. "I thought we were going to practice this morning." I pulled my straw out of my pocket and held it up.

Flea made a snorting noise. If Erma were here, she'd have told him that if he did that enough times, he'd suck his brain down his throat. But the look on his face told me now was not a good time to quote Erma.

"Not today, Captain," Wesley said, but his voice got kind of caught up on the word "Captain."

I slipped the straw back into my pocket. "Okay," I said. "Another time, then, I guess?"

Flea stood, brushing off the back of his pants. He made the snorting sound again.

"My sister says if you keep making that sound . . . ," I started, but trailed off when I noticed the other two boys stand and brush off their backsides as well. They all looked at me with dead eyes that made words wither up like decade-old petrified raisins in my throat. "I mean. Yeah. Maybe another time." I turned my attention to the toe of my shoe, which was making the world's most interesting design on nothing at all.

"Maybe never," one of the boys said. I couldn't remember for sure, but I thought his name was Buckley and his unique gift was smashing people until they could fit into a Dixie cup. Or martial arts. Something like that.

"Maybe," the other boy said. I was pretty sure his name was Colton and his gift was memorization, a pretty normal gift for a place like Pennybaker School. Too normal. He had probably memorized the entire dictionary or the periodic table. In French. "Maybe who thinks about spitwad wars at a time like this?"

I blinked. "Huh?"

Owen stood, too, and straightened the bowl on his head. Now Wesley was the only one sitting. "It's just that today of all days, nobody is really going to be thinking about much of anything except . . . you know."

"I do?"

"The head," Wesley said. "Mrs. Heirmauser's head." Out of habit, all five of them placed their hands over their hearts and gazed toward the door. Then a look of extreme sadness swept over each face. "We just can't really think about trivial things while it's missing."

"Trivial?" I said, surprising even myself by how passionate I suddenly felt about the spitwad war. It wasn't so much the war as it was . . . well, it kind of was about the war. It was about it being the only thing at this school that made me feel like I fit in. The only thing I could totally relate to. The only thing I wanted to be part of here. Plus, the idea of being responsible for lodging saliva-covered things in girls' hair sounded pretty great. I took a deep breath, certain that they wouldn't understand any of this. They all loved it here. They fit right in here. "I mean, of course it's not as . . . important . . . as the head of horr—as the missing artwork. But wouldn't Mrs. Heirmauser want us to move on? Wouldn't she want us to buck the system, to go forward with our childlike hijinks, to have fun in the way only the youth of today can? Wouldn't she have wanted us to forget all about her and do something to enrich ourselves, something that could better our, um . . . our aim, and our . . . our teamwork? Wouldn't she have been all about teamwork? Wouldn't she want the show to go on?"

When I stopped talking, they were all staring at me as if squirrels had just flown out of my nose. I quickly checked my bow tie. I'd improved my tying skills, but not by that much, and there was still always a possibility that it looked like a medical issue. They eventually turned their stares to each other, transmitting some unspoken communication.

"No," Flea said. "She wouldn't."

"Definitely not," Owen added.

Finally, Wesley stood. "Listen, Thomas. You're new and all; I understand. But the thing is, Mrs. Heirmauser was not someone who supported childlike hijinks. Some people say she was never a child herself. That she was born a math teacher." He held out a hand as if to stop me, although I wasn't saying anything. "I know, it sounds far-fetched. Unless you actually knew her. If you knew her, you could see it, I swear." The other boys continued nodding. "And Mrs. Heirmauser was a lot of things," he continued.

"Revered," Flea supplied.

"Loved by everyone in the town," Owen agreed.

"A genius," Colton said.

"And really smart, too," Buckley added.

Now Wesley turned his hand toward them. "She was a lot of things, but she was definitely not a champion of teamwork. She was about doing your own work, always. You probably never looked at the little plaque attached to the base of the statue, but it says, 'Eyes on your own paper, students.' A direct quote."

"Her favorite one," Owen said.

"Okay, okay," I said. "I get it. So we don't have the practice here. We move our practices to Pettigrew Park. You know, the one over on Nineteenth Street? There's a great climbing wall there that we can use for target practice. Surely Mrs. Heirmauser didn't have anything against parks."

"I don't think—" Wesley began, but this time I held out my hand.

"As captain, I insist. The war will go on. Practice will be at Pettigrew Park. Tomorrow, high noon. Be there." I waved my duct-taped straw in the air to show them that I meant it, and then vanished it into thin air.

Colton, Buckley, Owen, and Flea shook their heads and went back inside, leaving me alone with Wesley.

"What about . . . you know," I said.

"What?"

I whispered. "Following Reap. We're still going to do that today, right?"

Wesley opened his mouth to say something, but before he could get any words out, the bell rang, and we raced for class through the silent, morose halls.

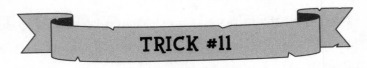

TRICK #11

THE SHADOW TRICK

For the rest of the day, Pennybaker School seemed like a totally normal school. The most depressed, heavy-sighing, tearful normal school in the world. Everyone seemed to leave their unique talents at home. Nobody was designing wearable microwave ovens or telling knock-knock jokes in ten languages or walking on their hands. Even Mr. Faboo left his Napoleon costume at home.

You would think I would have liked it, but I kind of hated it.

It was unsettling. Like I was sitting in a classroom full of aliens. I didn't know what to do with these people. I didn't know what to expect. I only knew that nobody dared say anything that might remind everyone of Mrs. Heirmauser, because the natural tendency to turn with hand over heart kept resulting in tears. I had no idea how often someone referenced the great math teacher until everyone stopped doing it. It was like nobody had anything to talk about anymore.

I tried at least a hundred times to catch Wesley's eye during Claymaking. He had acted so weird this morning, and we still hadn't devised a plan for following and catching Reap. If I didn't know better, I would almost think Wesley was avoiding me. I coughed, I hummed his favorite song from *Annie*, I even bumped into his desk when I walked past to get a hunk of clay.

Nothing.

Meanwhile, Reap seemed plenty nervous, looking over his shoulder every few seconds. Licking his lips a lot. Jumping whenever anyone made a noise. His project was all wadded up into a shaky lump. Although, to be fair, all our projects were wadded-up lumps. There were no gifted artists in my Claymaking class—which was probably why Miss Pancake sat with a bag of frozen peas on her head all the time.

I made sure I had my work station cleaned up and all my things put away before the bell rang so I could meet up with Wesley and get into snooping position. But the second the bell rang, Wesley shot out of his chair like a rocket and practically ran out of the classroom.

What was going on?

I followed him out into the hall, hissing his name, doing that fast-walk thing you do when you want to run but don't want teachers to catch you doing it and make you stop so they can yell at you about safety. Even so, he was still faster. He never turned around. The gap between us lengthened, until he darted around a corner and out of sight. Clearly, he didn't want to follow Reap anymore.

I turned back just in time to see Reap scurry out of the classroom and head straight for the cafeteria. Which was weird, because we had already had Meat and Greet.

I stood in place for a minute, unsure what to do, my vest inching up and pushing my bow tie into a beard. I took a breath and yanked it down. Fine. Wesley didn't want to help anymore. I would just have to be the hero all by myself. Wesley would be sorry he ditched me when I was getting all the glory.

I went back into the classroom and gathered my things. Miss Pancake had removed the frozen peas from her head and now rested with her face pressed directly onto her desk. More kids began to file in for sixth-period Claymaking. I should have been heading to Futuristic Arts, but I had other plans.

Like Reap, I headed for the cafeteria. Only instead of going all the way in, I hid behind the door and tried to pretend I didn't see the dead cricket on its back in the corner. I guessed the cricket had eaten the meat loaf. Poor guy. He should have been warned.

I tried to be as silent as possible, although it felt like my heart was beating loud enough to hear it outside of my body.

The tardy bell finally rang, and the hallways slowly got quiet. It wouldn't be long before someone noticed I was missing and started doing things like checking the bathroom stalls and calling my parents. I hoped Reap did something soon.

Just when I had convinced myself I had missed him, there were soft footsteps. I peeked through the crack of the door and saw Reap creeping out of the cafeteria with his hands stuffed deep in his pockets. I held my breath as he passed through the doorway, waited for him to get a few steps ahead, and then followed, walking on my tiptoes, shimmying behind a trophy case and ducking behind a book cart, praying the last button wouldn't pop off my vest and smack him in the back of the head.

Reap moved surprisingly quickly. I could barely keep up as he crossed the foyer, opened the front door, and slipped out. I counted to ten and then followed, pressing my back against the door. I could feel a lion head pressing into the top of my skull. It made me shiver.

I scooted to the left. No Reap. I scooted to the right. No Reap. I sprang off the door, rubbing the top of my head, and went down the stairs. No Reap, no Reap, no Reap.

Where in the world had he gone?

I paced the sidewalk a few times, and was just about to give up and go back inside when I saw a bush in front of the school jiggle just the tiniest bit. I froze and squinted. Maybe it was just my imagination. Maybe one of the lions had come alive and was waiting for me in the bushes. Maybe the meat-loaf cricket was actually undead and had followed me outside. Maybe the bush was coming alive . . . and was hungry. The bush jiggled again, a little more forcefully.

Or, maybe, the cause of the jiggle was Reap.

I tiptoed to the hedgerow and squatted, trying to see through the foliage. I couldn't see anything but leaves.

The bush jiggled again, and I jumped up so fast I nearly fell over. Wesley had the right idea. He was happily studying Futuristic Arts while I was out here about to get sucked into a bush. But then I heard a voice. A very Reap-like voice. Murmuring behind the jiggling bush.

It was now or never.

"Aha!" I shouted, pushing through the bushes and landing in a little clearing on the other side.

"Aaah!" Reap shouted, falling back into the brick wall behind him.

"I've caught you red-handed," I said, spitting out a leaf. "I knew it was you all along. Thief! Dirty, rotten, sneaky thief! Coming out here to hide your . . . bread?"

Sure enough, there was a large bag of bread on the ground where Reap had just been crouching moments before. It was open, and a slice had fallen out onto the ground.

"Please don't tell," Reap said.

"But where's the head?" I asked, still not understanding what I was seeing.

"The what?"

"Huh?"

"What are you talking about?"

"What are *you* talking about?"

He gestured toward the bag. "The bread. If you tell, I'll get in trouble, and so will Mr. Tony."

"Who's Mr. Tony?"

"The one who's been giving me the bread." He pulled himself back up into a crouch and stuffed the spilled slice back inside the bag. "From the cafeteria." When I still didn't comprehend, he said, "Mr. Tony? The guy who works in the kitchen? He makes the bread."

I pinched the bridge of my nose. "Just to be clear. You're saying 'bread,' not 'head.' Right?"

"Why would I be talking about a head?" And then it seemed to dawn on him. "Oh, you mean the Heirmauser bust. You think I stole it? Like, put it in my shirt and carried it out here into the bushes? So I could, what? Talk to it when I was lonely?" He laughed.

"Well, the thought had crossed my mind, maybe, a little," I said. He laughed harder. I scowled. "Well, it's not like stealing bread makes any more sense."

"Sure it does. Watch." He motioned for me to crouch

next to him, then tugged a hunk of bread off and started making a strange clicking sound with his mouth.

"What are you—"

He waved his hand at me to cut me off.

"You know, I'm getting pretty tired of people shush . . ." But I trailed off when I saw a pair of eyes. And then another. And another.

Reap kept making his clicking noise, and slowly, slowly, a prickly bunch of quills emerged from within the bushes.

"Is that a—?"

Reap nodded. "Hedgehog. I've named her Harriett." He offered Harriett the bread, which she quickly snapped up. "And those are her babies. I haven't named them yet. I'm still learning how to tell them apart." He scattered more lumps of bread, and a line of smaller hedgehogs crept out. One bypassed the bread and immediately went for Reap. He scooped it up and held it. "Usually I try to give them vegetables, because that's what they really like, but this week all Mr. Tony had was bread. They don't seem to mind it."

He kept talking, but all I heard was the buzzing of unholy cuteness blotting all the smart out of my brain. I felt like I had stepped into a fog of happiness and candy and hugs. I had completely forgotten about the Heirmauser head or Wesley ditching me or catching Reap doing something illegal. I lowered myself to the ground and sat cross-legged. Reap did the same.

I reached into the bag and grabbed a hunk of bread, then held it out until Harriett came over. She sniffed it, then began nibbling. I smiled so hard my ears hurt.

"So, you're not going to tell?" he asked.

I shook my head. "No. But I don't get it. Why hide?"

Reap cast his eyes downward, looking very ashamed. "It's my unique gift," he said. "Making friends with animals. They follow me everywhere I go. I can sort of . . . talk to them . . . in their language." He made a couple of clicks and a squeak with his mouth and Harriett paused, squeaked in response, and went back to eating. "She thinks you're scary."

He was clicking at animals, and *I* was the scary one?

I scratched Harriett's head with my finger so she would see I wasn't dangerous. "So? Isn't that why you're here? To show off your unique gift? We all have one." Sort of. I, of course, only had a Grandpa Rudy.

Another baby hedgehog abandoned the bread and scampered to Reap, quickly burrowing into his pant leg, then turning around and staring out at me happily from inside. "That's the thing." He pulled the baby out of his pant leg and put it in his lap with the other. "My dad went here. My uncles went here. My grandfather went here. All with the same unique gift."

"Animals?"

His face went white. "Sort of." He covered the ears of the babies in his lap and whispered, "Taxidermy. My grandfather specialized in eyeball reconstruction."

"Gross!" I yelled, causing Harriett and three babies to duck under the bush again. I lowered my voice. "Like, actual eyeballs? On actual animals?"

Reap nodded grimly. "They expect me to follow in their footsteps. I don't want to disappoint them. I'm pretending I don't have a unique gift at all, and hoping they'll let me go to Boone Public instead." My heart squeezed at the mention of my old school. Why hadn't I ever thought of just pretending I couldn't do magic? Sometimes I could make easy things really complicated.

"So you hide your gift and steal the bread and take care of your animals in private. And you had nothing to do with the missing head."

"Nothing at all. Please don't rat me out."

I sighed. "I'm not going to tell anyone."

He beamed. "Thanks, Thomas. I don't care what everyone else is saying about you. You're pretty all right."

"Thanks. I think you're pretty all r—" I blinked. "Wait. What do you mean, what everyone else is saying about me?"

"Here, you want to hold one?" He offered me one of the babies. An obvious avoidance tactic. And one that worked. Because, seriously, it was so cute I almost needed to lie down for a while. I took the baby, and Reap made a few squeaking noises at her. She sniffed at me, staring intently with her beady little eyes. I raised her up and touched my nose to hers. She didn't smell the best, but what can you expect with wild animals? She probably thought I didn't smell the best, either. "She's my favorite," Reap said. "She so nice and friendly."

"You should name her," I said. "Think of the nicest, friendliest person you know, and name her after that person."

He thought for a minute, then brightened. "I know!" he said. "I've got the perfect name for her."

I rubbed my fingers along her quills, careful not to get stuck. "What is it?"

His smile was so big it looked like it might break his face. "Helen!" he said. "Helen Heirmauser Hedgehog."

Oh, brother.

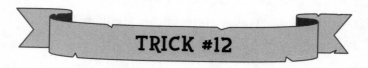

TRICK #12

THE BROKEN PENCIL

When I got home, I went up to my room and locked the door. I changed into a T-shirt and jeans, letting my sandpapery brown vest and tie crumple into a corner of my bedroom. The weekend was officially here, and I wouldn't have to look at that stuff for two days. Bliss.

I got down on my knees and reached under the bed, dragging out Grandpa Rudy's old magic trunk.

It had been a while. I hadn't noticed, but the fact that my magic was what sent me to Pennybaker School made me kind of hate it a little. And the fact that Owen, Flea, and Wesley—not to mention Chip Mason—asked me nonstop to show them my tricks made me hate it even more.

But as soon as I opened the trunk, I remembered that I actually really loved magic. The inside of the trunk smelled like Grandpa Rudy—spicy and sweet at the same time, with a little undertone of smoke and black licorice. It was a smell I imagined Houdini had; the scent of magic. It was a smell that made me want to do some basics. Oldies but goodies, Grandpa Rudy called them. Tried and true.

I picked up a deck of cards, worn and soft from years of being shuffled. "You see, Tommy," I said aloud in my Grandpa Rudy voice. "The thing about magic is, people will see what they want to see." I shuffled the cards using just one hand, the way Grandpa Rudy used to do. It was a move that had taken me a whole summer to learn but really impressed people when I did it correctly. I split the deck and spread it out in an arc across the floor. "So you have to make them want to see *magic*. Make them look away from the trick."

I held a card between two fingers and turned my hand, and it disappeared. I reappeared it behind my back.

"So much of successful magic," I said, doing a double lift, and then doing it again, "is about practice. About being so good, so smooth, that nobody will question you." I did a pinky break. "They. Will. Believe."

When I was a kid, I would sit at Grandpa Rudy's feet for hours and watch his hands so closely that my eyes got dry and felt like they would fall out of my head.

But even though I would watch with everything I had, I still would never see the trick. I would only see the magic. I was floored every time he passed two metal hoops through each other or pulled a toy out of an orange or made a glass of milk disappear. How did it happen, and why couldn't I see it, even when I was looking?

I supposed that was why I was so interested in learning the tricks after Grandpa Rudy died. I wanted to be the one to know there was no magic there. I wanted to do the tricking.

After a while, I got bored with practicing my sleight of hand and decided I would try something more challenging. I had once seen Grandpa Rudy pass an index card through a pencil. I was pretty sure I knew how the trick was done, but I'd never tried it myself.

Grandpa Rudy would have someone from the audience come up on stage. He would give them a pencil and have them check it out to make sure it was a real, whole, intact pencil. While he was doing this, he would tell them a story around the cigar he liked to chew while performing, about how he was in a special government program during the war, and how they taught him to use just about anything as a weapon.

"Tell ya what," he'd say, taking the cigar out and laying it on the table (where about eighty percent of the time it would burn a hole into Grandma Jo's tablecloth and make her start yelling when we got home). "I'll prove it to ya." He'd pull an index card out of his jacket pocket and hold it up. "I'll bet you I can break that pencil in half, using only this index card." He'd have the volunteer inspect the index card to make sure it was an ordinary index card. He'd then tell them to hold the pencil nice and tight, count to three, and . . . *boom*. Pencil broken. "See?" he'd say, retrieving his cigar and popping it back into his mouth. "Trained to use anything as a weapon." And then he'd make a joke. "You should see what I can do with a carrot," or "I once fought off a whole village with a single blade of grass," or "Now, hold your arm out real straight, and I'll get a bigger card."

What I loved most about those kinds of tricks was that even the volunteer helper had no idea how it was done. They were part of the trick and still didn't see the trick happen. Because they weren't looking for it. All they saw was the magic.

I dug through my desk until I found a stray index card and an old pencil. I just needed to find a volunteer.

I found Erma on the couch, watching one of her dumb teenage-girl drama shows, as usual.

"Hey, Erma," I said.

"No," she intoned, without even looking up from the TV.

"I just need some help real quick."

"No," she repeated.

"It's for a—"

"No," she said, louder. "And hush, I can't hear my show." This again. Sisters were no help at all.

I went into the kitchen, where Mom and Grandma Jo

were trying to make dinner, although that wasn't so easy with the two of them still being mad at each other.

"I'm just saying, it's a low blow to steal someone's skateboard," Grandma Jo said, furiously peeling a potato into the sink.

"I don't know what you're talking about," Mom said, but she was talking so lightly that it was obvious she was the culprit. "I didn't steal anyone's anything." She stirred something in a pot. "Besides, you were going to break your neck on that thing, and someone had to do something."

"I knew it was you!" Grandma Jo cried, pointing at Mom with the potato peeler. *Louis XIV: Peeled by a potato peeler. Snuffed by a spud.* "A woman's board is her best friend. You are a best-friend stealer!"

"I said I don't know what you're talking about," Mom yelled back, stirring faster and faster until stuff started to slop over the sides of the pot. "And I did you a favor by getting rid of that thing!"

This was quickly turning into a Mother-Daughter Potato Skateboard Smashdown Adventure, so it was definitely not the right time to ask either one of them to help me. I turned and wandered around until I was back to Erma.

"Where's Dad?" I asked.

"On his way home," she said, still not looking up, even though it was now a commercial.

I sighed and plopped into the recliner. I was tired of

doing card tricks by myself in my room. I didn't want to watch a bunch of girls fight and cry and put on lipstick on Erma's show. And the kitchen wasn't a safe place to be. I had no homework. I had nothing to . . .

Just then I noticed movement outside the front window. I slid over to the love seat and parted the curtains.

Chip Mason. Of course.

He was running through his front yard, wildly swinging a net. He swooped one way and then another, then leaped, stumbled forward a few steps, and kept running. Then he ran too close to the big oak tree and tripped over a root. He fell, his head torpedoing right into the net on the way down. He struggled for a few seconds to free himself, then just lay back, his chest rising and falling with deep breaths as he stared up into the sky.

I wondered what he'd been trying so hard to catch.

I wondered how tightly he could hold a pencil.

Sighing again, as dramatically as I could, even though all the drama I could muster couldn't take Erma's attention away from her show—in which someone had lied to someone else and another someone had let the lie slip, and now all the someones were slamming doors on one another—I pulled myself off the love seat.

It was pretty nice outside. Still warm enough for shorts, but not for much longer. Summer would soon be giving way to fall, and something about knowing that I would be heading into the Christmas season at Pennybaker School made it all the more permanent to me. It was depressing.

"Hey, Chip," I said, standing over him once again.

"Oh, hi, Thomas," he said, pulling himself to sitting.

I hated to even ask this, but, "What are you doing?"

"Nothing, really," he said. "Trying to capture something, but I'm not having much luck." He picked up his net and inspected it.

"What are you trying to capture?"

He stood, letting the net dangle by his side. "No idea," he said, offering me a huge smile. "I won't know until I capture it."

This, oddly, made more than a little bit of sense, and the fact that it did kind of scared me. I didn't know for sure, but I suspected that once someone got to understand a guy like Chip Mason with no further explanation, things were looking pretty doomed on the You're Weird Now, Too, Buddy scale.

"Wouldn't it be cool, though, if I caught a dragon?" he said.

"You mean a dragonfly?" I asked.

"No. A *dragon* dragon," he said. "One with scales and fire and everything."

I nodded slowly. "Yeah, Chip. It would be cool." *It would also be a miracle, since dragons don't exist*, I thought, but I didn't say it out loud. There were just some dreams you didn't crush for a guy. "Hey, I don't suppose you'd be willing to help me with something."

Chip's face brightened. He dropped his net to the ground. "Sure," he said. I could tell he was making an effort to keep cool about it, but he was failing miserably. He cleared his throat, looked down at the ground, and then looked back up at me with a very serious expression. In a low, "manly" voice, he said, "I mean, what can I do for you, Thomas?"

I held out my pencil. "I need you to hold this for me."

"Okay!" He didn't even ask why. Just took the pencil and held it as if it were made of gold. Which was probably something I should have really liked about Chip Mason—when Erma was telling me to hush because she couldn't hear her show, and Wesley was telling me I didn't understand things, Chip was all in, all the time—but it actually kind of annoyed me. *Don't do it just because I asked you to*, I wanted to shout. *Resist, man! Be a little bit difficult at least!*

But I didn't say anything. Just positioned his hands so he was holding it the same way Grandpa Rudy always positioned the hands of his volunteers.

"So you didn't know this about me," I began, "but when I was in the war—"

Chip lowered the pencil. "What war?"

I rolled my eyes impatiently, pulling his hands, and the pencil, back into place. "World War Two, I guess. Now, when I was in the war, the government taught me—"

Chip lowered the pencil again. "Not possible. World War Two took place from 1939 until 1945. Your parents weren't even alive yet. Your grandparents were probably babies. Grandfather Huck wasn't even in elementary school yet."

I raised the pencil again, his hands trailing along. "I don't mean I was literally in the war. Now. When I was in the war, the government taught me—"

He lowered the pencil again. "Well, I suppose it's possible for one to be figuratively in a war. I mean, tug-of-war doesn't technically involve any sort of munitions or force of arms. Of course, unless you mean literal arms, like the ones on your body. Which you definitely use when playing tug-of-war. Only in that case, it would literally be a war again." He cocked his head to one side. "Oh. But what about when two celebrities are having a flame war? I believe that is a figurative sentence all the way around, because there is neither literal flame nor literal war going on in those circumstances. Wouldn't you agree?"

I had totally forgotten what I was even out here for. "What?"

He held the pencil back in position. "Carry on."

Reluctantly, I went back to making a show of aligning his hands just so. "So, as I was saying . . ." I drew a blank. "What was I saying?"

"You were in the war. The figurative war, of course. Although World War Two was quite literal. And I contend that, while it is possible to be in a figurative war, it is really not possible for one to be figuratively involved in a literal war. But carry on. We shall suspend disbelief for the sake of the tale."

I dropped my hands to my sides and sighed. "Forget it."

He thrust the pencil toward me. "No, no! Keep going! I want to hear your incogitable war story."

I stared at the pencil for a second. It seemed so silly now, breaking a stupid pencil while talking about being a trained weapon. Grandpa Rudy wasn't a trained weapon. He was a guy with kind eyes and a soft laugh who loved cigars and Bill the rabbit and didn't mind his grandson sitting around watching him practice his magic all the time.

And I was definitely no trained weapon. I wasn't even sure what I was trained at anymore.

I sat in the grass, letting the index card I'd brought out flutter to the ground next to me. "Nah, it's a dumb trick," I said. "You hit the pencil with your finger, which is hidden behind the index card. That's what breaks the pencil. Not the card, the finger. And it probably hurts."

Chip Mason looked completely crestfallen that I'd told him the trick. He stared at the pencil as if it were the one at fault. Finally, he sank to the grass next to me.

"Oh."

We sat in silence for a few minutes, Chip picking blades of grass and, one by one, inspecting each blade, as if he expected to find a treasure on one of them. Which, knowing Chip, he probably did.

I was starting to think maybe I would go inside and practice sharpening my spitwad skills out my bedroom window, when Chip said, "So what do you want to do?"

"Huh?"

"You know. Do. What do you want to do?"

"With you?"

He nodded. "Sure. I've got my playing socks on." He kicked off one shoe and showed me what appeared to be a totally ordinary white sock beneath. "Mom's got Huck at the eye doctor, and I've already done all my schoolwork today. I'm free for the afternoon, and I'm feeling rather footloose about it."

"Footloose?"

He nodded again, eagerly, and then stood and did a little jig in the grass. "And quite fancy-free, too!" He jumped to the side and clicked his heels together.

"Why do you talk like that?" I asked.

"Like what?"

"You know. 'Quite fancy-free, too.' That's weird."

He blinked thoughtfully. "What's weird about it?"

"Nobody talks like that. Nobody even knows what it means."

"I know what it means," he said.

"But don't you care what kids your age think of you?"

He squatted next to me again. "Not really. Should I?"

Before I could answer, there was a screechy voice to my left. "Thomas Fallgrout, looks like you're hard at work doing nothing, as usual."

A terror on a banana bicycle seat, Erma's best friend, Arthura Crabbe, stood on the sidewalk in front of us, straddling her lavender bike, the glittery pink handlebar tassels blowing in the breeze. A helmet chin strap squeezed into her cheeks, making her face look even more pinched and angry than usual. Her cheeks squished and squeezed around a piece of bright blue bubblegum, which Arthura was always chewing, her glittery pink lip gloss sticking to it as it passed by her lips. Arthura wasn't my biggest fan, but Dad always told me that with girls that age, the meaner they were, that meant the more they liked you. Which made me not her biggest fan, either.

"Hi, Arthura," I said, without enthusiasm.

"I heard about what happened at your school," she said. She placed her hands on her hips haughtily.

Chip Mason perked up. "What happened at your school?"

I ignored both of them.

"My mom was talking all about it," Arthura said. "Mrs. Heirmauser was her favorite teacher of all time, ever." She said this last bit accusatorily, as if I were somehow involved in who Mrs. Crabbe got for teachers when she was a kid.

"She was everybody's favorite teacher," I said, trying to

keep emotion out of my voice. I didn't want to give Arthura any reason to keep talking to me.

"What happened?" Chip repeated. We both ignored him.

"Yeah," Arthura said. "She was everybody's favorite. Which makes it so weird what happened, don't you think?"

"I guess," I said. "I haven't really thought about it. I had never even heard of the lady until I started going to that school."

Arthura's eyes narrowed, and her pinched cheeks strained against the helmet strap gleefully. The blue gum shone from between her teeth. "That's what I thought," she said.

"What's that supposed to mean?" I asked.

"What happened?" Chip asked again.

"Nothing," Arthura and I said in unison.

"It doesn't mean anything, Thomas Fallgrout," Arthura said on a grin. "It doesn't mean anything at all. I'm sure whoever did what they did probably had no idea what a big deal it was when they did it. But he will for sure know soon. They'll catch him. And then he'll pay." Her face got hard and intense. "My mom cried when she talked about it. A lot of people are crying. Sure is unusual when you see someone who isn't crying, isn't it?" She scootched back onto her bike seat and lifted one foot to the pedal. Her face changed to total innocence. "Is Erma home?"

It was my turn to narrow my eyes at her. I didn't know if she was saying what I thought she was saying, but whatever she was saying, it sure seemed like she was saying it to me. Did she think I stole the head? But why would I?

"Sure," I said, studying Arthura Crabbe very carefully. "She's inside. Go on over."

Two teeth flashed between her squeezed cheeks. "Thanks, Thomas Fallgrout. Have a good day."

She hopped all the way onto her bike seat and started pedaling, easing out of Chip Mason's driveway and across to ours. I watched as she got off, removed her helmet, shook out her hair, and skipped up our walk to the front door. After a few seconds, Erma appeared, and Arthura disappeared inside our house.

After a beat, Chip turned to me. "Hey, Thomas?"

"Yeah, Chip?"

"You never said. What is it people think about me that I should be so worried about?"

I grunted with frustration. "Nothing, Chip. Just forget it. I've gotta go."

Before he could argue, I swept up my pencil and index card and walked back home, wondering how I would avoid Mom and Grandma Jo and Erma and Arthura until Dad got home.

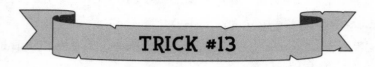

TRICK #13

POOF OF SMOKE AND THE GHOST CAT APPEARS

Pettigrew Park was the actual center of Boone County and was the hub of all things play. There were baseball diamonds and tennis courts, playgrounds, spraygrounds, skate parks, shelters, fields, running trails, and soccer goals. Everyone went to Pettigrew Park.

But today, Pettigrew Park wasn't looking so much like a hub. In fact, it was looking pretty empty. Way emptier than I expected it to look, especially given that I had told the guys to be there at noon to practice, and not a single one of them was there. I was the captain; they were supposed to take me seriously.

I took a seat on the merry-go-round and pushed myself in circles with my feet. I pulled out my straw and studied it. I wasn't sure why this was suddenly so important to me, but it was, especially since things had gotten so weird with the missing head and all. I smoothed the tape around the straw, pulled out a wadded knot of paper from my pocket, and popped it into my mouth.

So nobody was going to show up. Okay. I could deal with that. But just because they weren't practicing didn't mean I couldn't practice.

Still spinning, I raised the straw to my mouth and pushed the spitwad into it with my tongue. I waited until I'd made a few revolutions and chose a target—a pine tree on the edge of the playground. I took a deep breath and spit with everything I had.

I missed.

But not by much.

I chewed up another piece of paper and tried again. I missed again, but then the next time I hit the tree with a *thop*, right in the center of the trunk. It was great, so I did it again. And again. Next thing I knew, I had forgotten all about everyone standing me up at the park, I was having such a good time. I started experimenting with doubles—*thop thop*—and then triples—*thop thop thop*. I worked my feet in the dirt to spin the merry-go-round faster and faster, so fast I almost couldn't see the tree as it whizzed by. I loaded up again, took a deep breath, and . . .

"Gross!"

I planted my shoes in the dirt so hard it almost pulled me completely off the merry-go-round. I slowed to a stop, but not slow enough for my eyes to catch up with the rest of my body. The world was swoopy and out of focus. I turned myself toward the sound of the voice, and my vision sharpened on the form of Patrice Pillow, who was standing right next to the pine tree, wiping a spitwad off the center of her forehead.

Louis XIV: Spitwad sniper demise. Lethal lugie.

"Sorry," I said. "I didn't see you there."

"I guess not," she said. Her face was all scrunched up in a way that reminded me of Arthura Crabbe in her bicycle helmet.

"I missed my target," I said.

"Well, it's good to know I wasn't the target. Nasty."

She wiped her palms on her skirt and then brushed her hands together as she walked toward the merry-go-round. She sat next to me. I wasn't sure what exactly was going on, but when she started to dig her toe into the dirt and turn us, my stomach started to feel a little wonky. Too much spinning. Too much girl.

"So it's true, then, huh?" she asked.

"What's true?"

"That you're still insisting on having the spitwad war. Despite, you know, *everything* that's happened."

I picked up my feet and sat cross-legged, scooting back so I was in the center of the merry-go-round. "Well, why not? I mean, I don't get it. It was just a statue."

She dragged her toe and we skidded to a stop. She turned and shook her head at me. "You have to quit talking like that."

"Like what?"

"'Just a statue.' It will make people . . ." She pressed her lips together.

"Make people what?" I slipped my straw back into my pocket.

She ducked her head. "You know . . . suspicious."

I stared at her, and she sighed.

"Listen, Thomas. I wrote this story once. It was about this newlywed couple, and they were being haunted by the ghost of a feral cat."

"A cat," I repeated. "Really? Who gets haunted by a cat?"

She socked me in the shoulder. "Hush; you're missing the point. This cat was really making their lives miserable.

Things were going missing, doors were closing on their own, noises in the dark, that kind of thing. And the wife, she was starting to lose it. Like, really lose it." She swirled her fingers at her temples in the universal motion for "crazy." "But the husband, he was doing okay, you know? He was just going on about his life like normal. He couldn't understand why his wife was so freaked out about this cat. He told everyone that nothing was going on. That his wife was the problem. But it turned out *he* was the cat from the very beginning."

She stared at me meaningfully.

"I don't get it," I said. "The guy was a cat? Like a shapeshifter or something?"

She rolled her eyes. "No. Why does everyone say that?" She slapped her palms on her knees. "The guy was the one doing the haunting."

"So he was dead?"

She grunted and whacked her knees again. "No!"

"Well, how could a live guy be a ghost? Don't ghosts, by definition, have to be dead?"

"He wasn't an actual ghost. He was doing things to make it appear that the cat was haunting her." She looked like she'd had to explain this way too often.

"So I'm a guy pretending to be a cat," I said. "I still don't get it."

"You're not a . . . You aren't pretending . . . Ugh; just

forget it. Forget I said anything." She stood up, and the merry-go-round turned slowly from her movement. "I shouldn't have bothered to come here."

That was when it dawned on me, the whole point of her cat story. I slid to the edge of the merry-go-round and stopped it. "Wait. So you're saying people think *I'm* the one who stole the head of horror?"

She closed her eyes like she was in pain. "You shouldn't call it that."

"Sorry. The statue. You think I stole the statue?"

She shrugged. "I was just telling you a ghost story. It's my unique gift, remember? Just like yours is making things disappear."

I stood. "Okay, there are a lot more magic tricks than just making things disappear," I said. "There are card tricks, sawing people in half, lots of chemistry tricks, making things appear . . . wait. I can make things disappear. So people *do* think I stole the head. Why would I want that horrible thing?"

"You shouldn't call it that," she said again. "Actually, I need to go. My mom wanted me to come home for lunch." She edged away from me like I was a hungry grizzly and we were alone in the forest.

"But you have to convince them," I said, following her. She sped up. "You believe me, don't you?"

"See you at school, Thomas," she said, and jogged down one of the paths into the woods.

"I'm not the ghost cat! I'm not!" I yelled, but she was already gone and didn't hear me.

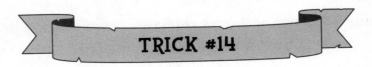

TRICK #14

CHAINED TO THE THUNK

I spent extra time on my tie on Monday morning, pulling it into a perfect knot, yanking on the edges until they were stiff and straight. They tickled each side of my chin every time I moved.

Louis XIV: Deadly tickle fight. Worse, nondeadly tickle fight with Erma, who tinkled every time someone touched her armpits. (Trust me. I learned this the hard way.)

I also brushed my hair carefully, using water and some of Dad's gel to smooth it down over my forehead. I even gelglued the cowlick flat on the back of my head. I pulled out a clean white shirt (the one I'd been saving for second semester) and used Mom's sewing kit to attach two buttons to my vest. They weren't the real buttons—as far as I knew, my vest's real buttons had been in the basement of Pennybaker

School since my first day, when they popped off and rolled down the stairs. I'd replaced one with a green button from Grandma Jo's old coat, and the other with a pearly white button from one of Erma's old Easter dresses. But at least my vest buttoned, and if I held my books carefully in front of me, nobody would be any wiser.

I washed my face and brushed my teeth and even rinsed with mouthwash. A guy couldn't make a good impression with zombie breath.

All finished, I stood back and studied myself in the mirror. I looked . . . pretty much the same, except my tie-wad wasn't so waddy and didn't look as much like a blob of brown mold growing out of my chest. I let out a gust of air I'd been holding.

"Useless," I said to the mirror. I popped off the buttons and threw them in the trash.

"What was that?" Dad was standing in the doorway, his morning coffee in hand like always.

"Do I look like a ghost cat to you, Dad?" I asked, turning one way and then the other.

"A ghost cat," he repeated. He pondered, pooching his lips. "Nope. I'd say you look much more like a scurvy pirate. Or maybe a runaway lab experiment gone wrong." He made a monster face and then winked at me in the mirror, but when he saw that my expression didn't change (not to mention, I didn't even bother to make my fingers into a pirate hook at all), he got serious. "What's up, pal? What's a ghost cat, anyway?"

"He's a guy who tries to make everyone think everything is normal so he can drive his wife crazy," I said, pushing past him. I picked up my backpack, which was leaning against the wall next to the stairs.

"I didn't know you were married. I'd have bought you a gift," Dad said, following me. We reached the bottom of the stairs, and he put a hand on my shoulder and turned me to face him. "Really, you're not making any sense. Is everything okay?"

I nodded, then shook my head, then nodded again. "I guess so. It's just that Mrs. Heirmauser's head is missing, and I think maybe people think I took it."

Dad's hand fluttered near his heart involuntarily, all joking instantly over. "Yes, I heard about this heist. Such a shame that someone would do that. Everyone in the town loved Mrs. Heirmauser. She was the best."

"So I hear," I mumbled, heading toward the kitchen, which was eerily missing the sound of Mom and Grandma Jo bickering. I could smell sausage. My stomach growled.

"I don't understand, though. Why would people think you took it?"

"Arthura thinks he took it," Erma said. She popped an orange slice into her mouth and smiled an orange-rind smile at me.

"Shut up, Erma," I said, sliding into my chair.

"Thomas," Mom scolded. "Don't tell your sister to shut up."

I piled sausage and scrambled eggs on my plate. "Fine. Erma, be quiet or I'll spit in your juice."

"Not much better," Mom said.

Erma pulled the orange slice out of her mouth. "Blah blah blah blah blah," she said, to prove that when Mom was around, she didn't have to be quiet just because I told her to. And that she wasn't worried that I would actually spit in anything.

Dad sat next to me. He was holding his briefcase in his lap, and he had his suit coat on. "You didn't answer me," he said. "Why would people think you took the Heirmauser statue?"

I bit into a sausage and shrugged. "I guess because I don't get why it's such a big deal. That head was gruesome."

Mom gasped and dropped a spatula. Dad flinched, and a wave of coffee splashed out of his cup and onto the kitchen table. Grandma Jo chuckled.

"See? He totally took it," Erma said. "Arthura's very intuitive." She stuck another orange into her mouth and opened a book, her legs swinging under the table. She didn't even notice the look of fear everyone was giving me.

"Thomas," Mom said in a low, ominous voice. "Did you take Mrs. Heirmauser's statue?"

"Who knew the little guy had it in him?" Grandma Jo

136

added. Still giggling, she ruffled my hair. I tried to duck away. I'd spent all that time gelling and combing for nothing.

"Mother!" Mom scolded. "This is no laughing matter. That statue is very important to the history of Boone County. Whoever took it is public enemy number one right now."

"Cool," Grandma Jo breathed. "You're a celebrity, Tommy!"

Wait. Public enemy number one? I wasn't sure exactly what that meant, but it sounded really serious. I had wanted to be number one at a lot of things in my life, but "public enemy" was definitely not one of them. It sounded kind of dangerous. And lonely.

"I didn't take anything," I said, dropping my sausage onto my plate. I looked around. Everyone was staring at me as if to say, *Of course, that's exactly what someone who stole something would say.* "I swear! I didn't even like that thing. It creeped me out. Why would I want to take it? Don't you guys believe me?" I looked around the room. Nope, they didn't believe me at all.

Finally, Dad cleared his throat and took his coffee cup to the sink. "Of course we believe you, pal," he said. "If you say you didn't take it, then we"—he glanced at Mom—"have to believe you." He rumpled my hair, too, but suddenly I didn't care as much. "Have *to believe you*," he'd said. Not "*want* to," not "*do*," but "*have* to." If I couldn't even look innocent to my family, what was the point in trying to prove my innocence to a whole school full of strangers?

I had a feeling I was about to have an Everyone at School Hates You, You Lying, Stealing, Liary Stealer Adventure.

Just like before, Wesley wasn't waiting for me in our usual spot in the vestibule. There were a few kids hanging around, most of them whispering to each other while they peered at the pedestal. Principal Rooster had put on a curly brown wig and bent behind it so that his chin was resting on top, posing as Mrs. Heirmauser.

If the original statue had been scary, this was the stuff night terrors were made of.

"What's going on?" I asked a boy who was passing by. He opened his mouth to answer, but when he turned and saw who he was answering to, he snapped it closed again and raced away, taking the stairs two at a time.

Samara Lee and Dawson Ethan were standing nearby, their heads pressed together.

"What's he doing?" I asked, butting between them and gesturing toward Principal Rooster.

They both flinched and then gave each other meaningful glances, before Samara crossed her arms haughtily and said, "Wouldn't you like to know?"

"Yeah. That's why I asked."

She cinched her arms tighter around her chest. "Well, we're not going to tell you. Traitor."

I stumbled back a step. "Traitor?"

"Samara," Dawson hissed in a warning-type voice.

Her eyes grew wide; his eyebrows went up in response. Her lips pursed. He tilted his head down and gazed at her under lowered brows. She huffed. He puffed. They were having a whole conversation with their face muscles. Which would have been kind of awesome if they hadn't been talking about me. The traitor. Finally, Samara's arms went straight by her sides, her fists clenched, and she growled.

"Fine," she said. "Principal Rooster is trying to make everyone feel better by doing a re-creation of the stolen statue." She put extra emphasis on the word "stolen." "But it's not working, because everyone knows that he's not the real Mrs. Heirmauser. And nobody feels safe with a thief walking freely among us." This time, she put extra emphasis on the word "thief."

I wanted to argue with her, to tell her that I was no thief and that I was just as upset about this as everyone else—which, okay, I wasn't, and probably everyone knew that, and that was precisely the problem—but before I could even open my mouth, she grabbed Dawson by the wrist and pulled him away. They went into the office, where Miss Munch was lying on the floor with a cold compress across her eyes.

"Oh, yeah? Well, I don't feel safe with a thief walking among us, either," I said, but nobody was listening to me. They were all too busy whispering to each other about me.

I glanced back at Roostermauser. Was it just me, or was he showing a few more teeth than he had been a moment ago? And had the angry crease between his eyebrows gotten deeper? I shivered and headed toward class.

7

I wound wearily through the desks in Facts After the Fact. It had been a long day. Nobody was really talking to me, though it seemed like everyone was kind of talking about me. Someone had written an essay entitled "The Untrustworthy Stranger" in Lexiconical Arts and dropped it on my desk. Someone else had written the words *GIVE IT BACK* on my locker. Wesley, Owen, and Flea ate lunch in the library, so I sat alone at our table. Someone stole my banana cream pie while I was buying a second milk to go with it.

It didn't take a genius to see that Arthura was right and Patrice was right and Mom was right—I looked guilty, everyone thought I'd stolen the head, and I was public enemy number one.

Fortunately, I had my crew in Facts After the Fact class. I was looking forward to an hour of spitwad practice. I hoped Mr. Faboo was wearing his George Washington wig. It made a great target.

"Hey, Wes," I said, plunking my backpack on my desk.

Wesley didn't respond. He didn't even look up from the

picture he was drawing, although I could tell by the way his fingers were jerking and his hair looked kind of sweaty around the ears that he wanted to. I snapped my fingers in front of his face. He didn't budge.

"I tried to catch you before following Reap, but you took off. How come?" Silence. "It was a false alarm, anyway. He didn't do it." More silence. "Hello? Earth to Wesley?" Nothing. I tried quoting his favorite Shakespearean play, *Hamlet*, which I had known absolutely nothing about before I met him but practically knew by heart now. I clenched my fist, raised it high in the air, and made my voice melodramatic-deep. "My day has been bad, but . . . that it should come to this!" I cried out, which I thought was a pretty good effort, but, aside from the slightest pause of his colored pencil, barely even registered with Wesley.

"Okay," I said. "I get it. Don't speak to Thomas today. Fine. Whatever."

I started to slide into my desk when Flea appeared out of nowhere, flanked by Buckley on one side and Colton on the other. They all had their arms crossed.

"You're about to be sitting in my seat," Flea said. He was trying to look tough but only managed to look slightly twitchy.

"What are you talking about? This is my seat. I always sit here."

"Not anymore," Flea said, and the two boys on either side of him shook their heads slowly, menacingly. "I sit here now."

We stared each other down. I could have flicked Flea a hundred yards with my little finger if I wanted to, but I figured that the day everyone decided that Thomas Fallgrout was uniquely gifted at being a bad guy was not the best day to be flicking littler guys anywhere.

"Fine," I said, moving my backpack to the desk on the other side of Wesley.

Buckley sidestepped so that he was standing in front of that desk. "That one's mine."

"Since when?"

Colton stepped in front of the empty desk just behind Wesley. "And this one's mine."

"You sit by the window," I said, pointing. "Clear over there."

"It's mine," he repeated. "No head-stealers allowed."

"I didn't steal anybody's head," I said exasperatedly.

"The head-stealer desk is over there," Flea said, pointing to the desk in the far right-hand corner of the room. The one pushed so far back it was wedged into Fern Corner with the broken projector and the extra Kleenex supply. The one nobody ever sat in, not even the new kids. We protected them from that chair.

It was the one-short-leg chair.

"No way," I said. "I'm not sitting in the short-leg chair."

Buckley and Colton took a step closer to me.

"Wesley," I said. "Tell them." But he simply hunted through his pencil box, as if I hadn't spoken to him at all. "Oh, come on."

Buckley and Colton closed in as Flea luxuriously stretched out in my rightful chair, crossing his arms behind his head. I sighed, resigning

myself to an hour of *thunk*ing, *thunk*ing, *thunk*ing every time I made a move. Sneeze, double-*thunk*. Erase something, *thunk-thunk-thunk*. Start to doze off, *thunk* with a feeling of falling that would jerk you awake with your heart in your throat. It would drive a man mad, all that *thunk*ing.

"Okay. But when you all find out who really took that statue, you will owe me the biggest apology," I said.

But now they were sitting quietly in their own chairs, looking like kings on thrones. I slid into my chair as carefully as humanly possible, barely breathing . . .

. . . barely moving . . .

. . . just a little . . . to . . . the . . . left . . .

Thunk.

"Gah!" I went for broke, pulling things out of my backpack with wild abandon. *Thunk-thunk-thunkity-thunk*. And just when I sat up straight again—re-*thunk*—out of nowhere, a spitwad flew through the air and stuck itself right on my earlobe. I peeled it off and threw it on the ground—*thunk*—disgustedly. "Who did it?" I practically yelled.

Everyone stayed facing straight ahead.

Slowly, Wesley turned around, his eyes dead, his face serious. "When sorrows come," he recited in his Shakespeare voice, "they come not in single spies, but in battalions."

I was no Hamlet expert, but even I could guess what that meant.

Everyone at Pennybaker School for the Uniquely Gifted was against me.

Thunk.

TRICK #15

SLEIGHT OF FAMILY

Erma had a dance recital after dinner. Normally, Mom and Dad would have made me go to the recital to "support my sister," "be a team player," and "let Erma know the whole family is behind her," but this time they were noticeably silent at the dinner table. Erma was wearing eye makeup and lipstick, and her hair was pulled up so tight her eyes looked kind of squinty and her mouth didn't shut all the way when she chewed. Otherwise, I'd have had no idea it was recital night, because nobody mentioned it at all.

"When are we leaving?" I asked when Mom stood up to clear the plates from the table.

She and Dad gave each other a funny look. Dad cleared his throat. "Well, pal," he said. "We thought that maybe this one time you could stay at home."

"Work on your homework," Mom added brightly. She took my plate to the sink, which was filling up with suds.

"I don't have any homework," I said.

"Excellent." Dad wiped his mouth with his napkin and tossed it onto his plate. "A free night off. What a nice treat, huh?" He nudged my shoulder with his knuckles.

"But what about supporting my sister? Being a team player?" I could barely believe the words were coming out of my mouth, because normally I would have been begging to be left home alone while they went to one of Erma's boring recitals, but it was the fact that they weren't telling me I had to go that was upsetting. It was one thing to let me off the hook; it was another thing to not want me there. "What about letting Erma know that the whole family is behind her?"

Mom gave Dad another look. Dad licked his lips, took a drink, and then scooted his chair back from the table. "Look, pal," he said. "I just don't know if it's a good idea right now to . . . Well, it's just that with everything that's . . . You see, we don't want to invite any . . ." He glanced at Mom, and another strange look passed between them. Mom sighed, her eyes going hard and determined.

"Erma, why don't you go upstairs and get your ballet shoes?" she said, taking Dad's plate from the table. Erma scurried out of the room as Mom dropped the plate into the sink. She turned back and started wiping the table with a rag. She was wiping really hard and fast, the way she always does when we're about to have a You're Pushing Me to the End of My Rope Adventure. "Thomas, what your father means to say is that with everything that's going on right now—with the missing statue and everything—it may not be the best time for you to be immersing yourself in big crowds of people who have kids at Pennybaker School. Or who went to Pennybaker School. Or who knew anyone who went to Pennybaker School. Basically everybody. Especially not at times when your sister has worked very hard and would be very sad for things to get ruined. Accidentally, of course." She stopped wiping and laid a damp palm across my wrist. "You understand what I'm saying, right?"

"Not really."

She stared at me for a second, then picked up the rag and began scrubbing again. "Your grandmother is going to visit some old friends at the nursing home this evening. You should go with her," she said.

"But Dad just said I got a free night off."

She turned back to the sink. "That was before we had this conversation."

"Dad? Tell her." But Dad wouldn't meet my eye. He was probably afraid of having a You're Getting on My Last Nerve Adventure with Mom, too. "Dad?"

He finally lifted his eyes, guiltily. "Thomas," he said. "People are talking."

I looked back and forth between Mom's back and Dad's forehead, which was pointing toward the table again, and tried not to notice that Dad had just called me "Thomas" instead of "pal." Was I no longer his pal? "So you're making me go with Grandma Jo because people think I stole that dumb head out of that dumb school's dumb hallway?" Neither of them answered. "Do you think I did it? Mom? Dad?"

"Oh, well," Dad said, "It's complicated . . ."

"No, of course not . . . But did you?" Mom asked at the same time.

"Why would I want it?" I asked, standing up. "Where would I hide it?"

Mom turned from the sink and placed her fists on her hips. "That's not exactly a no."

"No," I said. "There. You happy? I didn't take Mrs. Heirmauser's head. Now can I go to Erma's boring recital?" My mouth was such a betrayer. I needed to take it outside and run over it with Grandma Jo's skateboard.

"I'm sorry, Thomas, but you can go with Grandma Jo instead. Look at it as an adventure!"

"Great," I said. "A So Bored I Want to Eat My Own Dentures Adventure."

But it didn't really matter what I had to say about it. Anyone who knew my mom knew that once she had made up her mind, it was completely impossible to change it.

Mom finished cleaning the kitchen while Dad got his

going-out-on-a-weeknight pants on, and before long they were gone. I was left sitting at the kitchen table, levitating the salt shaker, because I honestly had no idea what to do with myself now that I'd been banned from the recital. Banned from the *family*.

After a while, Grandma Jo came in. She was wearing her bright red lipstick—the shade she always wore when she was "going someplace respectable"—and a blue flowery dress with slip-on thick-heeled shoes. Grandma Jo never wore dresses. Whoever we were visiting must have been pretty important to her.

"So I hear I have company tonight," she said, picking up her purse and dangling it delicately over one arm.

"I guess so," I said in a glum voice.

"Good," she said. "You'll make a good alibi."

"What do you mean?"

Just then there was a honk outside. "Barf's here," Grandma Jo said. She opened her purse and pulled out a couple of knee pads and some gloves with padded palms. She bent and unrolled a pair of pantlegs under her dress and kicked off her shoes. "Let me get my sneakers, and we're out of here. You might want to bring a helmet or something."

"Wait," I said, getting up and following her halfway down the hall. "Barf's taking us to the nursing home?"

"Not a chance," Grandma Jo called from her bedroom. She came out in a pair of black sneakers and had slipped off her dress, revealing a black long-sleeved shirt with a grinning skull on the chest. "Do I look like the kind of person who likes to hang out in a nursing home?"

"Mom said you had a friend there."

Grandma Jo waved me away. "My friends are too young for nursing homes. Plus, my friends are awesome. You're about to meet one. Come on, don't lollygag. Parkour awaits."

"Parkour?"

Grandma Jo cocked one hip to the side and gave me the same look Erma gives me right before she calls me a Big Dumb Duh. "Jumping off things and walking on the edges of other things." She mimicked someone running and then flying with her fingers. "Really high things."

"Jumping off . . . wait. I'm pretty sure Mom wouldn't approve of you doing that," I said.

Grandma Jo came to me and put an arm around my shoulders. "Listen, kid. Your mother doesn't approve of me doing anything but eating applesauce. Don't tell me you like the way she's treating you right now. Like you're some kind of criminal. Your own mother, suspecting you of stealing the most hallowed head in all of Boone County. If a guy can't trust his mother, who can he trust?" She was walking me toward the door the whole time she said this.

"I can trust her. She doesn't really think I'm guilty."

But when I thought about it, Mom definitely seemed to think I was guilty. And Dad did, too. The way he wouldn't look into my eyes. The way they didn't want me to be in a crowd of people from Pennybaker School. The way Mom acted all nervous around me since the day the head went missing.

Grandma Jo was right. If I couldn't trust my own mother, who could I trust?

A guy named Barf who liked to jump off buildings, that was who.

"Okay," I said. "Let me get my bicycle helmet."

"Besides," Grandma Jo said to my back as I headed toward the garage. "Barf knows a guy. If we need to make a fake statue appear, we can do that. I got your back, kid."

I paused.

Even Grandma Jo thought I was guilty.

Suddenly jumping off buildings didn't seem like the scariest thing in Boone County.

"Actually, Grandma, just go without me," I said. "I don't feel so good anymore."

TRICK #16

OUT OF NOWHERE, A PLAN IS HATCHED

By Tuesday, it was very clear that my best option was just to keep my head down and do my schoolwork. Everyone was mad at me, including Grandma Jo, whom Mom caught sneaking in after a full evening of jumping off things and walking on the edges of other things.

"Some alibi you make," Grandma Jo had huffed as she carried her knee pads to her room. "You couldn'ta made up something?"

"Sorry," I'd said—something I felt like I was saying all the time these days. Which was weird, because, other than just not liking Mrs. Heirmauser's head, I hadn't done anything to be sorry for. And I wasn't entirely sure I needed to be sorry about that, either.

Somehow I made it through another day, even though I was still sitting at the uneven desk in Facts After the Fact class.

"So, Thomas Fallgrout," Mr. Faboo said, leaning over my desk. "Have you decided on the subject for your Nationwide History Day project?"

Thunk. "I was sort of thinking Louis XIV," I said, and then wanted to pull my tongue out and impale it on a rusty fork. *Impaled on rusty eating utensils.* But my mouth wouldn't quit talking. "I thought maybe I could research the history of the necktie. I could call it 'Louis XIV's Necktie Adventure.'"

He pursed his lips and squished them around on his face from one side to the other. "Been done."

"Really?"

He nodded. "Twice, actually, two years ago. The first one was clearly superior, but then again Angus Mack's unique gift was fashion design. He could tell you the difference between lawn cloth and lampas without batting an eye. He was a clear favorite for the project. Besides, there really is nothing interesting about Louis XIV, who, quite coincidentally, was—"

"The first to wear a necktie for fashion, I know," I finished for him.

"Have you considered something a little more unique? For example . . ." He swept to one side and gestured toward a red-haired boy in the front row. The boy was sweating profusely as he wrestled with two long, squeaking balloons. "Harvey Hinkle over there is working on Henry Maar. The Sultan of balloons." Harvey Hinkle gave the balloons another twist and one popped. A girl squealed. Harvey's shoulders slumped.

"How about Harry Houdini? Since my gift is magic and all."

Mr. Faboo leaned over me again. "Think outside the history book, Thomas Fallgrout."

He started to walk away, and in a panic I blurted out, "The history of the cheese puff!" I could see Wesley's back stiffen. *Thunk-thunk.*

Mr. Faboo stopped walking and turned. "Intriguing." He stroked his chin. "Edward Wilson at the Flakall Corporation. Yes, yes. Where would we be without his delicious invention? Brilliant, Thomas Fallgrout! With that kind of thinking, you could have a real future in history."

Working out that sentence made my brain hiccup, but it sounded like it was probably a compliment.

"Carry on!"

Thunk.

As soon as Mr. Faboo's back was turned, Wesley spun around in his chair.

"That was my idea," he hissed.

"So? You gave it to me," I whispered back. *Thunk-thunk-thunk.*

He pointed at me with his pencil. "I did not give it to you," he said. "You stole it."

"I did not!" *THUNK!*

"Did too! But I guess I shouldn't be surprised. Seems like a lot of things have been stolen since you got here." Not true. Only one thing had. But it didn't seem like a good time to argue with him.

"You know I didn't steal that statue," I said. "I was the one who wanted to catch Reap, remember?"

"Yes, how convenient that you just happened to see Reap 'walking out of the school with something under his shirt.'" He used air quotes. "Can you say 'misdirection much'? *Magician?*"

"Are you saying I was trying to frame Reap?"

He held up his palms. "I'm only saying that it's pretty handy that, even though the whole school was standing right there, you were the only one to see Reap supposedly steal something."

I never wanted to break a promise so bad in my whole life. But I had given Reap my word that I wouldn't tell a soul about Harriett and the baby hedgehogs, so I had to keep my mouth shut. "Whatever," I said, going back to my paper. "It's my brilliant topic now, and I'm using it. No matter who came up with it."

He narrowed his eyes at me and leaned farther over the back of his chair. "I'm watching you, Thomas Fallgrout," he said in a gangster voice.

"Yeah," Buckley said, using a voice that was probably supposed to be Threatening Gangster, too, but only really sounded like Seasonal Allergy Mucus. "You better watch your back."

Thunk.

17

"You look like you've had a bad day," Mom said when I slid into the car. "Your tie is especially, um . . ."

She seemed at a loss for words. I pulled down the visor and looked in the mirror. The knot part of the tie had gotten swiveled all the way around to the back of my neck. It looked like the buns Erma wound her hair up into when she went to dance class. I yanked it around to the front, then loosened it and pulled it off angrily.

"Never mind," I said. "My day was fine."

Mom acted like she wanted to say something more but seemed to think better of it and just drove us home. I turned on the radio to fill the silence but didn't listen to anything coming through the speakers. All I could hear was the stuff inside my head: *"You stole it." "I'm watching you." "You better watch your back."*

"You know," Mom finally said as she pulled into the driveway, "it's never too late to make things right. You realize that, don't you, Thomas?" She turned off the car and gazed at me, her hand still on the keys, which were dangling from the ignition.

"I guess," I said, though I wasn't exactly sure what she was getting at.

"You can always apologize if you've hurt someone's feelings or ask for forgiveness if you've made a mistake. Or, you know . . . return something that you might have accidentally taken." Her voice got quieter and quieter as her sentence went on, probably because she could see my face getting frownier and frownier with every word.

I didn't hurt anyone's feelings or make any mistakes, and I haven't stolen anything! I wanted to yell. But it seemed pretty pointless to say anything at all, so instead I just opened my door. "I'm going to see if Chip can hang out," I said.

I know. I couldn't believe it, either.

It was just that Chip was the only person who didn't seem to be accusing me of anything these days.

17

As usual, Chip was outside when I got there. Only he wasn't *outside* outside. He was more like hanging outside. From his bedroom window. On the second floor.

He was sitting on the window ledge so that one leg was dangling down the side of the house, his back against the window frame. He was holding a pizza slice. And using it as a microphone. For an opera song.

I tried to wait until he was done, but opera songs are apparently really long. And horrible. Like the-sound-of-something-dying-under-the-sea horrible. *Louis XIV: Operatic octopus obliteration.* I ended up having to interrupt him.

"Oh, hey, Thomas!" he said, waving with his whole arm—the one not holding the pizza. He wavered a little from the motion, and I half expected him to fall all the way out and land in the bushes below. Something else for the whole world to blame me for. "I'll be right down."

He disappeared inside his bedroom, and a few minutes later popped through the front door, the pizza half-eaten now, a slick of orange grease trailing down his chin.

"You're just in time for act two. It's very exciting. The whole thing is a telling of the infamous Tomato Revolution of 1616. Act one sets up the romantic interest between Sir Pepper Roni and his fair maiden, Mozzarella. It's lovely, but theirs is a forbidden love, and soon the evil temptress Mary Nara sweeps in and causes all kinds of problems. In act two, Mary almost gets away but is captured by Lieutenant Incisor in a rousing duet—note I said duet, not diet." He laughed the stuffy kind of man laugh Dad uses when we run into someone from his work at the grocery store. "The Molar Prison aria is quite beautiful. Would you mind taking the harmony?" He opened his mouth wide to begin singing.

"Chip," I said. "Just eat your pizza."

His mouth clopped shut, and then he shrugged and took a bite. "Okay. But you'll be sorry to miss the finale. A four-part harmony led by the olives. I suppose you'll have to wait until the show comes back on tour next pizza day."

"I think I can do that," I said. I plopped down on his front porch and rested my chin on my hands glumly. "I have nothing better to do but wait."

He sat, gazing at me thoughtfully and stroking an invisible beard. "I'm not wearing my psychology socks," he said, "but nevertheless I'm beginning to pick up on a mood change with you today."

"What?"

He took another bite of his pizza. A hunk of pepperoni was now stuck in the grease on his chin. "You seem sad," he said.

"Oh. That. Yeah."

"Might I inquire what has your normally balanced brain chemicals in an unstable predicament?"

"Are you asking what's wrong?"

He nodded. "To put it colloquially, yes."

I shook my head and rolled my eyes. Why I was sitting here on Chip Mason's front porch, getting ready to spill my guts, I had no idea. But even before my mouth opened and stuff started coming out of it, I knew I was going to do it. Because even though Chip was weird and I never understood anything he had to say, he was willing to listen. And right now I really needed a friend who would listen.

"Someone stole this bust from my school," I said.

"Oh, yes. I heard about that," Chip said. He nibbled on his crust before tossing it into the yard. Two birds immediately went after it. "The head of the late, great Helen Heirmauser, correct?"

"Yeah. Some bronze sculpture of her screaming."

He held up a finger. "Actually, it was most likely a copper and tin alloy."

I paused. "Anyway—"

"Although I suppose it could be any mixture of metals. Could include nickel, lead, iron, or even zinc, perhaps. Though it's most likely copper and ti—"

"Do you want to hear the story or not?" I interrupted.

He tucked his hands under his thighs and lowered his head. "Go on."

"So someone stole the head, and for some reason, everyone thinks it was me. Well, not just for some reason. They think it was me because I called it a 'head of horror' a few times. And I said it was creepy. And I might have hit it with a spitwad once."

Chip, who'd begun to look increasingly concerned with every word that came out of my mouth, suddenly gasped. "That's bad," he said.

"I know. Thanks for pointing out the obvious. I just didn't realize everyone was so in love with the thing. And I still don't get why. But because I can do magic, everyone thinks I made it disappear. Like I can just tuck a giant head into my pocket without anyone noticing."

"Is that really how you make things disappear? You tuck them into your pocket?"

"Well, there's more to it than . . . you're missing the point, Chip. Even my parents and my Grandma Jo think I stole it. They won't let me go to Erma's recitals, nobody at school talks to me, and Mom's telling me to return it. But I don't have it. I don't even know who would!"

"Sounds like a real mystery," he said. He scuffed his shoes against each other. "Granted, I'm not wearing my sleuth socks, but it still has all the hallmarks of a mystery, so I feel confident in calling it that regardless."

"Yeah," I said. "I wish I could solve it so everything could go back to normal. Or to whatever normal is at Penny-baker School."

We sat in silence for a few minutes, the only sound the squeak of Chip's shoe soles rubbing together.

Suddenly, he turned to me, his face all lit up like it was Christmas morning. "Hey! I know!"

"What?"

"It's a whodunit, right?"

I nodded.

"And, while I may not be wearing them now, I do have mystery socks. I might even have a spare pair that you can borrow. And I'm pretty good at reasoning and problem solving and consider myself quite rational. Plus I've watched a lot of *Scooby-Doo*." He beamed. "What do you say?"

"What do I say about what?"

He started flapping his hands between us madly. "We could solve the mystery together."

"What mystery are you talking about? And if I have to wear funny socks, I'm out."

"The mystery of who stole the Heirmauser head. No socks required."

I chewed my lip. "I don't know . . ."

"Oh, come on, Thomas! It will be fun. We'll walk about the city peering at things through magnifying glasses, wearing disguises, having thoughtful yet charming powwows about clues that we've gathered."

I stood up. "I'm not having a charming anything with anyone."

He popped up next to me. He still had a lump of pepperoni stuck to his chin. "We'll find out who stole the head and return it to Pennybaker School. And when we reveal our evidence, people will have no choice but to believe that you didn't do it."

"I don't know . . . ," I said again, but honestly I wasn't sure what I was so hesitant about. As much as I hated to admit it, Chip Mason had a good idea. And he was right—when I brought the real thief to justice, everyone would have to admit that I was innocent all along. They would have to apologize. And maybe even throw a We, the Entire Town of Boone, Are Sorry, Thomas Fallgrout, for Ever Disbelieving You and Calling You a Liary Stealer, Because You Are Awesome and We Should Have Seen All Along That You Couldn't Possibly Have Been the One to Steal Anything Party.

Okay, so the party title could use a little refining, but the point was . . .

"Okay. I'll do it."

Chip jumped up and down with glee, seemed to catch himself, and instead held out one hand very solemnly. After a few seconds, I realized he wanted to shake on it. I took his hand in mine.

And I was officially solving a mystery with the weirdest kid in Boone County.

TRICK #17

IT'S ALL IN THE HANDS

The next morning, there was a snowstorm.

Which was weird in September. But, then again, every-thing was weird lately.

But, still a possible snow day is a possible snow day, and what better time for a snow day than when all that awaited you at school was silence, mean glares, and the short-leg desk? I raced to my window, threw open the curtains, and . . .

Never mind. It wasn't snow.

It was paper. A whole lot of saliva-coated little balls of paper. Spitwads. And my window was covered with them. Sometime during the night, or maybe early in the morn-ing, someone had used my window for target practice. A clear message that I was now the target.

"So this is how it is now, huh?" I said out loud, but nobody was listening, because I was all alone in my bedroom.

Quickly, I dressed in my uniform, making sure to slide my special team captain straw into my shirt pocket, just in case the message was that everyone had forgiven me, they all knew they were wrong to suspect me in the first place, and the boys versus girls war was on after all.

That wasn't the case.

I followed Owen and Flea around all morning, trying to figure out what was going on. They went about their day pretty much normally, except that every so often, they would pass each other in the hallway and make strange hand signals to each other, as if they were talking with sign language. Everyone else seemed to be watching me carefully, and I could have sworn I saw a few spitwad straws poking out of pockets, but I was too afraid to make eye contact with anyone long enough to find out for sure. I didn't want my face to be the next snowstorm scene.

I finally got my chance to really check things out during Four Square class. We were outside and were supposed to be running the trail that circled the soccer field, but most kids were standing around talking while Coach Abel chatted with Principal Rooster, who was still wearing his Heirmauser wig. Owen was wearing a soup pot on his head, the handle poking straight out behind him, and he and Flea were bent over one of Owen's computers, which was set up on a picnic table by the gym door. I snuck up behind them, pretending I had a cramp, and peered over Owen's shoulder.

Looked like plans to me. A map, maybe. Strategy. A square box labeled "Foxhole."

And beneath that a chart of hand signals and what they meant. Two thumbs up, "Fire at will." Two thumbs down, "We've been spotted." A strange forefinger/middle finger crossing thing, "Sniper." A single pinky in the air, "Bathroom break." Other hand signals meant things like, "Girl unprotected at two o'clock," "Medic," and, "Nurse Hale is coming. Abort mission! Abort mission!"

It took all I had not to gasp. They were having the spitwad war after all.

But they were having it without me. The captain.

Well, now I was just plain mad.

I caught up with Wesley in the greenroom after fourth period. He was wiping stage makeup off his face and only had one side done, making half of him look intensely surprised. He jumped when I came in, and held a tissue between us like a shield. He looked around the room, panicked.

"Where are your henchmen?" I asked. I could have said "Buckley and Colton," but "henchmen" sounded much more like something someone should say when face-to-face with his betrayer.

"Henchmen?" Wesley said, his lip twisting in confusion. "You mean Buckley and Colton? Dude, they're not henchmen. Buckley still sleeps with a night-light."

I wasn't sure if I was supposed to know that information, but I decided it could be helpful knowledge somewhere down the line.

"Listen," he said, holding out his hands, stop sign–style. "I don't want any trouble. I'm just taking off my Nicely Nicely face and then going to lunch."

"Lunch?" I said, moving in on him despite his outstretched arms. Not that I was going to do anything, but there was something kind of satisfying about making him worry that I would. "Or target practice?"

Now both sides of Wesley's face looked surprised.

I nodded. "Yeah. I know all about it. How you've decided to have the spitwad war without me. The hand signals you've created. Do you know what this symbol is?" I turned my thumbs down right in front of his face.

"We've been spotted?" he said in a quavering voice.

"No, it means traitor!" Although he was right. According to Owen's computer notes, it did mean "We've been spotted." "It means turncoat! Double-crosser! Back stabber! Benjamin Franklin!"

He lifted a finger hesitantly. "I think you mean Benedict Arnold."

"I know what I mean," I yelled, because sometimes

yelling could cover up getting embarrassing things wrong. "I'm going to give you another signal. Are you ready for it?"

He crossed his arms over his chest, his hands grabbing his shoulders, and leaned backward as far as he could over the makeup table. I made a bunch of ridiculous—and something I would never remember again—motions with my hands. A lot of fluttering and snapping and possibly the sign-language gesture for "kangaroo." I ended, strangely, by kissing the tips of my fingers, one by one, which I didn't want to be doing but which was one of those things where once you start, you've got to commit and keep going.

"I don't think I learned that one yet," Wesley said.

"Of course you didn't. I just came up with it." I slowly backed away from him, all sinister-like, toward the door. "But I'll tell you what it means. It means you have an enemy on that battlefield. A spitwad ninja. Someone who isn't playing for either side. It means you should be very careful out there, Wesley, because I'm going to be a team of one. And I'm coming for you." I almost paused to repeat that in my head. I didn't want to forget it, because it sounded like something someone would say in one of Dad's action movies, and I wanted to remember it forever, in the likely event that I would never get to make an awesome good-guy-going-rogue speech again. I started out the door, then had a thought and turned back. "Oh. It also means I'm not sitting in the uneven desk anymore. So . . . there."

I plunged out into the hallway, a weird lump forming in the back of my throat. I supposed I had realized it as soon as I saw the blizzard on my window. But after everything I'd just said, it was officially sinking in.

I wasn't just Wesley's enemy.

I was everybody's enemy.

Everybody, that was, except Chip Mason.

TRICK #18

THERE'S A PLAN BEHIND YOUR EAR

It took me an hour to scrape all the dried spitwads off my bedroom window. Now the bushes looked kind of Christmassy, but the window itself just looked . . . spitty. With each scrunch of my mom's ice scraper against the window, I silently vowed to sit up all night, if that was what it took, my special straw in hand and my window open just enough . . .

"Hey, Thomas," I heard, and almost fell off the stepladder I was standing on.

"Jeez, Chip, you scared me," I breathed. "You shouldn't sneak up on a guy like that."

"Sorry. But technically, I wasn't sneaking. Sneaking would require an intent to be silent for the purpose of not being detected. I just happened to be walking silently. And I said your name. Which means I was definitely not interested in not being detected." He held out a hand and bowed his head. "I know. Two negatives in one sentence. I'll write an extra paragraph in tonight's grammar reflection."

"That sounds like really boring homework."

"Oh, it's not homework. I just like to do it."

I turned back to my scraping. "What do you want, Chip?"

"I've been thinking." He sat on the bottom step of my stepladder, making me sway. I held on to the window sash. "The other day, when you were giving me the details of the pate peculation . . ."

"The what what?"

"The pate peculation." Chip looked testy. It was the first time I'd ever seen that look on him. "The head theft? 'Pate,' head. 'Peculation,' theft. I was trying to be creative."

I came down off the stepladder, forcing him to move over so I didn't step on him. "Look," I said. "If we're going to be hanging out together for this thing, you're going to have to start speaking English."

"That was English."

"Then you need to start speaking normal English."

He sighed. "Okay, okay, but that's not the point of what I was trying to say anyway. Can I finish?"

I dropped the ice scraper in the yard and sank down in the grass next to it. "Go ahead."

He took a deep breath. "When you were giving me details of how it all happened, you mentioned some curious things."

He poked a finger in the air. "One, you said one of the custodians fainted."

"Crumbs, yeah."

"And you said another one caught him. You used a name that I very much doubt was her given name, as most people don't name their children after housecleaning devices."

"Zelda the Mop. Get to the point, Chip."

"And you said a third custodian was out for the day."

I found a spitwad in the grass and flicked it with my forefinger. It ricocheted off the house and landed in the bush with the others. "So?"

Chip stood and started pacing. "So," he said. "You later mentioned that the principal was trying to re-create the statue, but before that, you said there was someone else messing with the pedestal it had previously been resting on, and his chin was right on the darker spot where the head had hidden the sunlight from the wood."

"Byron the Rat King," I said. "Yeah. He was polishing the pedestal."

"Or," Chip said ominously, leaning over me, "wiping off fingerprints."

"You mean—"

He nodded, excited. "Who other than the criminal himself would be wiping down the very pedestal that was the scene of a crime? And why else would he be wiping it down?"

"He was polishing it," I said softly, but I didn't sound convinced by my own words. Byron had been so quick about it once he saw me there. He couldn't get away fast enough.

"He was covering his tracks."

I opened my mouth to tell Chip he was crazy, full of silly guesses, and there was no way Byron the Alligator-Human Hybrid had stolen the head. But I couldn't deny that his theory made sense. Byron was strange, seemed to live in the basement, had been missing the day the statue disappeared, and was seen the very next day, wiping away what might have been the only evidence that could lead to the thief.

"That does seem suspicious," I said.

"I knew it!" Chip crowed, dancing around me. "I knew it! I knew it! I knew it!"

I stood up. "We should tell somebody, right? Principal Rooster? Maybe my mom? Yeah, my mom and dad." I started to walk toward the house.

"Wait!" Chip grabbed my elbow and pulled me back. He was surprisingly strong for such a small guy. "Not yet. We can't."

"Why not?"

"Because we don't have any proof. The legal requirement of burden of proof is on the prosecution, not the defendant." I gave him another what-are-you-talking-about look, and he let out a gust of frustrated air. "We can't just go around pointing fingers and saying he did it. We have to have proof that he did it."

"But he wiped that away," I said. "That's our proof."

"Our proof can't be there is no proof. But don't worry, I have a plan." He motioned for me to lean in closer. "We sneak into the custodian closet and find our proof there."

"Sneak in? How are we supposed to do that? Even if your mom lets you take a day off from school . . ."

"Let me worry about that. I'll wear my persuasion socks. She's putty in my hands when I wear those. It's not like anybody at Boone Public would miss me."

"Well, my teachers are definitely going to notice that I'm missing. Plus, what if Crumbs and Zelda the Mop are in the custodian closet when we sneak in?"

"You really need to stop calling them that. But . . ." He pulled me in even closer, so close that our noses were almost touching, which meant my back was practically bent in half trying to get down to his height. "We don't go during school hours."

I squinted. "You mean . . ."

"We go right now. You have a bike, don't you?"

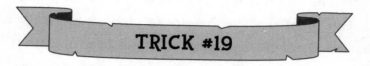

TRICK #19

HOCUS POCUS BATS AND NOISES

Of all the things I never thought I would be doing in this world, I especially never thought I would be breaking and entering into the school I didn't like with a boy I didn't like. Yet there I was, the sun starting to set and Chip Mason's hind end wriggling in my face.

"Did you get it yet?" I asked, wincing as his butt pressed up against my nose. His feet were in my hands. I was supposed to be giving him a boost, but he was a lot heavier than I expected him to be, and my hands kept sinking until I was cheek-to-cheeks with Chip Mason.

"Not yet; boost higher," he said from above. "I can't quite reach this last screw."

I grunted, putting all my muscle behind it, and lifted my arms. His shoes were digging into my palms, but at least his back pockets were no longer within breathing distance. Chip wiggled some more, there were a few soft metal scraping sounds, and then the ventilation grate from the boys' restroom fell past my face and landed in the ivy below.

"Got it!" he called. "Lift me higher!"

Even though I was already shaking and sweating, my interlaced fingers aching, I dug deep and lifted him higher. He pulled up onto tiptoes, teetered for a moment, and then hoisted himself through the hole where the grate had been. There was an echoey thud, a splash that sounded very toilety in nature, and then, "I'm in!"

"Shhh!" I hissed, looking over my shoulders. But one of the great things about Pennybaker being on the top of a hill was that I could see nobody else was anywhere around.

He opened the window next to the grate and poked his head out. "I'm in," he repeated.

"Now go to the door I told you about, and I'll meet you there."

The sun had dipped below the horizon, and shadows were inking the bricks surrounding the side door—what everyone called the recess door. Hidden by vines on one side and a line of trees on the other, it seemed the safest entrance into the school.

I heard echoey footsteps on the other side of the door and my heart quickened, my palms flooding over with sweat now. We were breaking and entering. This was a crime. The kind you saw on TV shows. If we got caught, we would be in huge trouble. Like, jail trouble.

But if nobody found the missing head, I could be in jail trouble anyway.

The latch on the door creaked and the door swung open, Chip Mason grinning on the other side. One shoe and pant leg were soaked.

"What happened to you?" I asked.

He looked down, then flapped his hands dismissively. "I landed in a toilet. No big deal. It was mostly flushed."

Mostly? I didn't know if I really wanted to walk around with a guy whose pant leg had been in a mostly flushed toilet.

"Come on." He motioned for me to follow him. "I saw the basement door over here. And you have to hear this."

Taking a deep breath, I stepped into the darkened hallway of my school. The door shut behind me with a loud click. It was done. I'd broken and entered. I might as well investigate now, so I could have a story to tell my bunkmate in prison. Chip was hurrying down the hall in front of me, his shoes making a *step-squish* sound.

But as we passed through the deserted vestibule and emerged on the other side, I began to hear something: a raspy growling noise surrounded by an odd twanging. Chip stopped short and cocked his head to one side.

"What is that?" I whispered.

He pointed toward the basement door, which was hidden beneath the stairs in a corner so dark you could have hidden every spider in Boone County back there. And probably some snakes. With bats for pets. I rummaged through my pockets in hopes that I'd stashed Grandpa Rudy's glow fingertips in there.

Grandpa Rudy used to enthrall me for hours on end, passing lights through his ears, up his nose, into his mouth, through his leg. It wasn't until after he died and I found his fingertips that I realized it was all sleight of hand, that he was turning lights on and off on his fingertips and making it look like the light was disappearing. I carried his fingertips around often, because you never knew when a boring moment might crop up and you could work on your own hand skills.

But I forgot that I'd been super mad when I changed out of my uniform and had been in such a hurry to get outside and start scraping off the spitwads that I'd forgotten to put them in my pockets. I was going to have to climb into the dark spider/snake/bat den without illumination.

The growl and twang was back, and Chip, who'd been reaching for the door handle, stopped short. His worried eyes were practically glowing in the dark.

"Do you think it's something alive?" he whispered.

"Well, I'm not sure if something dead is really a better option," I answered.

"Good point. Let's go in."

Before I could protest, Chip pulled open the door, exposing a steep wooden staircase and bare cinder block walls, which were covered with cobwebs. A single lightbulb hung on a string, swaying. The noise started up again. It was so much louder—and so much more chilling—than before.

"I just remembered something," I whispered. "I think I was supposed to be home for dinner."

Chip reached back and grabbed my arm. "Don't you want to clear your name?"

I did. I really, really did. We walked down the steps toward the noise.

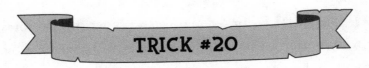

TRICK #20

TRICKED BY NAW

"NAAAW . . . NAAAW . . . NAAAWNAAAW . . ."

The noise only grew louder as we crept down the stairs and into the shadowy basement. Brooms and mops were lined up against the wall, looking like a creepy, skinny audience to whatever was going on in the far corner, behind the furnace. Mop buckets and shelves with rows and rows of cleaners and sprays and that powdery stuff they sprinkle on vomit stood in our path, and we had to wind around, every step making my legs wobblier and wobblier. I was starting to weigh how embarrassing it would be to hold Chip's hand for safety. Maybe worth it.

"NAAAW . . ." A grinding throat noise and a twang. "NAAAW . . . SAYNAAAW . . ."

"Chip!" I whispered. He didn't hear me. "Chip!" I whispered louder. He turned. "I think we should go."

He made a gesture with his two fingers at his eyes. "Look out for the missing head. It could be hiding anywhere."

"But what about that noise?"

He had already turned and was walking straight toward the very noise that he didn't seem to hear. I glanced around nervously, hoping I would see a glint of light bouncing off Mrs. Heirmauser's slightly misshapen nose and could get out of here before we found out what, exactly, was making that noise.

I was so busy peering into corners that I forgot to look in front of me. Chip had stopped short, and I didn't know it. I bumped into him from behind, sending him sprawling up against a stack of metal dust pans. It was probably a pretty small clang, but it sounded so loud that I pushed my hands over my ears and squinched my eyes tight.

"NAAAW—what was that? Who's there? Who is it?" the voice from the other side of the furnace boomed.

Positive: so the noise had been coming from a human.

Negative: a very angry-sounding human.

"Run, Chip!" I yelled, and made for the stairs, but I only got a couple of steps before I felt something grab the back of my collar. I yelped. "He's got me! Save yourself! Call 9-1-1! Send my father! Tell my mom I loved her! Don't forget me when I'm gone! Heeelp!"

Chip sauntered into my line of vision, his fists stuffed

into his pockets. "It's okay, Thomas," he said. "It's just the custodian."

"But he's got me! He's going to steal me, too!"

"Simmer down now, kid," a voice said in my ear, only it wasn't as gruff and growly as it had sounded before. It was more . . . nasally. "I'll let you go as soon as you stop squirming."

You would think I would've stopped fighting then, but for some reason I didn't. I even looked at my feet with dismay as they continued to kick the air, little grunts and gasps coming out of my mouth. Chip and the custo-dian stood there

patiently, the grip on my collar never relaxing, until I finally just gave up, my body going limp. I was breathing hard.

"You done?" the custodian asked. I nodded. He let go of my collar, and I scrambled behind Chip. I realized I was looking at the same custodian I'd run into in the vestibule not that long ago. Byron the Basement Dweller. He put his hands on his hips. "Now, what are y'all doin' down here?"

"We're here to solve a mystery," Chip said proudly.

"Are ya now? What kind of mystery? Is that what that one meant when he said I was gonna steal him, too?"

"The statue," I said, pointing accusatorily at him over Chip's shoulder. My finger shook, which kind of took away from my point. "You stole the statue. We're here to get it back."

"You mean the statue from upstairs? I had nothing to do with that."

"Let's just check the facts, shall we?" Chip said, clasping his hands behind his back and getting a good pace going. I felt exposed as he walked back and forth, but I was happy to let him speak. "Fact number one: you were the only custodian left unaccounted for on the day the head went missing. Fact number two: you were spotted wiping down the pedestal the very next day." He stopped and faced Byron head-on. "Almost as if you were wiping off fingerprints. Fact three: you know the school inside and out, including the many places where one might be able to stash an ill-gotten artifact."

"Fact number four!" I said. I was getting into this.

Chip looked at me. "I don't actually have a fourth fact."

"Oh. Sorry." I gathered myself, then pointed at Byron again. "You're caught, red-handed. Now, tell us where the statue is."

To our surprise, instead of hanging his head and leading us to a dusty corner, Byron began to laugh. First a little giggle, and then a head-back howl. "You two broke in here because you think I stole the Heirmauser statue?"

"Didn't you?" I asked.

"The facts are the facts," Chip said.

"Yes, yes, well, y'all are welcome to search the whole basement over if you think it's down here. Feel free to clean the place up while you're at it. I've got work to do."

"What kind of work?" I asked. "School's been out for hours. I don't think you're supposed to be in here this late."

He raised his eyebrows. "And are you—the one sneaking around in the dark—going to tell on me? Won't they be interested in finding out how exactly you got into a locked school?"

"Oh, yeah," Chip said. "That reminds me. You might need a mop in the first-floor boys' room." He flicked a few drops of water out of his shoe.

Byron shook his head and started back around the big furnace, where he'd been when we got here. "See yourselves out before I call Principal Rooster," he said. "Who, by the way, was the one who asked me to polish the pedestal. So it would be nice and shiny for when the statue is recovered."

I followed him around the furnace.

"What was that noise you were making when we got down here? What is it exactly that you're hiding back . . ."

I trailed off as I saw what was behind the furnace. A small lamp on the floor, illuminating an open book. A beat-up metal folding chair. And, balanced on the seat of the chair, a guitar. Byron picked up the guitar and looped the strap around his neck. He strummed a few strings.

"Singing," he said. "I was singing. That was why I wasn't here the day the statue was stolen. I was auditioning for a country-and-western show. That 'noise,' as you call it, was me trying to learn a song. I'm having a hard time getting my 'naw' to sound right. NAAAW . . . NAAAW . . ." His mouth opened wide. He looked really ridiculous.

So ridiculous he had to be telling the truth.

"Let's go," I said to Chip, who had come around the corner and was making "O"s with his own mouth while he watched Byron struggle with his. "He didn't do it."

"But we haven't searched," Chip said.

"We don't need to. It's not down here. I believe him."

Chip's shoulders drooped. "Yeah. I guess I do, too."

"NAAAW . . . ," Byron growled from behind the furnace.

My eye twitched.

Louis XIV: Naaaw'd to death.

A CLUE APPEARS! RAZAMATAZZ!

I was no longer having an Uneven Desk Adventure, but Wesley had changed his Nationwide History Day project to "The History of Great Betrayers." And he was very loud about doing his research.

"Hey, Flea, did you know that the definition of 'betrayer' is 'one who disappoints the hopes or expectations of someone,' or 'one who is disloyal'?"

"Really?" Flea answered. "Does it say anything about taking things that don't belong to you?"

"Oh, you mean, like Nationwide History Day ideas and treasured art, maybe? No, it doesn't seem to say anything about that. But I haven't researched any specific betrayers just yet. Did you have any specific betrayers in mind?"

Oh, boy. I almost preferred the *thunk*ing.

I raised my hand. "Mr. Faboo?"

"Yes, Thomas Fallgrout?"

"May I use the restroom? It's sort of an emergency." A Stop Listening to Wesley Emergency.

"Come right back, please."

I darted out of the classroom, relieved to be in the empty hallway, where I couldn't see or hear anybody. I went to the restroom and did my business, but I still wasn't ready to go back to class yet. There were only about ten minutes left in the period—if I played my cards right, I could get back just in time to pack up and leave. I devised a plan to pretend the cafeteria's ham salad had demanded a lengthy bathroom stay, which would have been totally believable.

I didn't know where to go or what to do to pass the time, so I went to the fancy stair railing and listlessly ran my fingers along it as I walked back and forth around the balcony that looked down over the vestibule below. And the empty pedestal.

I wished I could see some obvious clue. Something that would blow the case wide open. Trophy case, office, health room, empty pedestal. Empty pedestal, health room, office, trophy case. Trophy case, office, health room, empty—

I screeched to a stop. Took two steps back. Leaned over the rail and squinted. Had I seen what I thought I'd seen? I squinted harder.

Bright blue. Dented up like a brain. Resting right on the base of the pedestal.

Looking left and right over my shoulders, I sprinted down the stairs, around and around and around until I was in the vestibule. Miss Munch was coming out of the office just as I stepped onto the landing. I didn't have a hall pass, and I was pretty sure neither Miss Munch nor Mr. Faboo would understand why I would need to use the restroom on the bottom floor when there was a perfectly good restroom right next door to our classroom.

I ducked under the stairs and held my breath, hoping Miss Munch wouldn't see me. She wandered through the foyer, reading a paper, paused next to the empty pedestal and began to place her hand over her heart, then seemed to remember that the head wasn't there and scurried away, patting the back of her hair. I pressed myself farther under the stairs, my eyes pulsing with my heartbeat and my lungs ready to explode. I waited until her footsteps faded away before I finally let out a burst of air, bending over with my hands on my knees while I panted away the black spots in front of my eyes.

Once I had my breath back, I edged out of the shadows, my eyes planted on the office in case Principal Rooster or Nurse Hale or Counselor Still were lurking about. The coast was clear.

I darted across the vestibule, straight to the pedestal, and fell to my knees.

Yes. Blue. Brainy-looking. Chewed gum smeared with slimy pink glitter.

A clue.

I searched my pockets for something to pick it up with. Chip would want to see this. No, Chip would *need* to see this. This could be the clue that solved the mystery. I had nothing—no paper, no Kleenex, no plastic bag. Only pocket lint and my special spitwad straw.

As much as it pained me to do it, I reached down and peeled the gum off the edge of the pedestal with my bare fingers. It had gotten pretty hard on the outside, but was still squishy underneath.

Which was gross.

But even grosser because I was certain I knew whose mouth this gum had been in.

I knew that slimy pink glitter.

What I didn't know was why Erma's friend Arthura would have been anywhere near the Heirmauser pedestal.

TRICK #22

NOW YOU SEE US, NOW YOU DON'T

I should have known when Chip agreed to meet me at the roller rink Saturday afternoon that he might show up in roller-skating socks.

"John Joseph Merlin invented the roller skate in 1760," Chip said, trailing behind me over the dirty carpet, a pair of skates hanging from one hand. "He actually invented what we would now call the inline skate, sort of like an ice skate with wheels for the blade. Did you know that, Thomas?"

"No."

"It wasn't until 1863 that the four-wheeled roller skate, called the quad skate, was invented. Do you know who invented it, Thomas?"

"No."

"James Leonard Plimpton. And only three years later, he rented out a hotel in Rhode Island, and do you know what he created in their dining room?"

"No."

"A roller rink! The first ever roller rink open to the public, in fact. And who knows, if he hadn't done that, we wouldn't have this roller ri—"

"Why do you even know this stuff?" I asked, whirling on him. "Nobody normal cares." He blinked at me but didn't answer, so I sat down and shoved my feet into my skates. The music was loud, thumping along with dancing lights and a disco ball, but there weren't many people there. Just a birthday party full of kids Erma's age and a few teenagers, who were coming out from the locker area, which was a darkened little alcove by the restrooms. The single fluorescent light in that corner had flickered on and off—mostly off—for as long as the rink had been open. Most little kids were scared of that corner, which made it a perfect place for teenagers to do teenager stuff. Chip delicately placed his foot in a skate.

I tied my skates and glided toward the alcove, trying to look nonchalant, even though I wasn't the best at skating and I was on edge about the gum. "Come on," I said.

Chip followed me, even though he only had one skate on—roll-*thump,* roll-*thump,* roll-*thump.* "And did you know that there was a man named Russell Moncrief who skated all the way across the country on roller skates in only sixty-nine days?"

"No." I rolled into the alcove and pushed myself into the farthest corner, wedged between a locker and the wall.

Chip stood at the very edge of the alcove as if he was afraid to come all the way in. He frowned. "I can't quite remember who holds the record for longest roller skating limbo, though. Shameful." He brightened and patted the side of the first locker. "But I can tell you who invented the locker—"

"Would you just get in here already? I have something I need to show you."

Chip roll-*thump*ed his way into the alcove. "This feels very clandestine," he said.

"Very what?"

"Secretive. The origin of the word clandestine is 'clam,' which is Latin for 'secretly.'" I stared at him. He stared back. "What?" he finally said.

"Are you done, Dictionary Dan?"

He nodded. "Probably not, but you may proceed."

I shifted over to one side and pulled a plastic bag out of my jeans pocket. He leaned forward, studying it carefully. "What is it?" he asked, poking at the gum through the plastic.

"I found it stuck to the bottom of the pedestal," I said.

He gasped. "Explosives?"

"What? No. It's gum. You mean to tell me that you know the name of the dude who built a roller skate a hundred years ago, but you can't tell the difference between a piece of chewed-up gum and a bomb?"

"Actually, if you do the math, it was more like two hundred fifty years ago." I shot him a look, so he squinted at the bag, then let out a breathy laugh. "Oh, yeah. That does look like gum."

"The thing is . . . I think I know whose gum it is. And you do, too, if you think about it. You saw a piece just like it being chewed in your driveway the other day."

Chip held out his hand, and I placed the bag in it. He looked at it through the swirling colored lights. He opened the bag and sniffed. He squished the gum between his thumb and forefinger. He put it up to his ear and listened. He pressed it to his forehead and closed his eyes. Then he repeated every step a second time.

"Well?" I asked, when I couldn't take any more of his stalling.

He held the bag out to me. "I have no idea whose that is," he said.

"Think about it. Pink bike, tight helmet, really annoying voice . . ."

Just then, a blur of purple and glitter rolled past the alcove, a shrieky laugh coming out of it. A new arrival at the birthday party. Arthura. I pressed my back harder into the wall, praying that she wouldn't look over at us and see us analyzing her gum. "Come awwwn, Erma," she said, around a wad of bright blue gum that looked just like the one in the bag that Chip was currently listening to again.

He grinned. "Yeah. Yeah, I hear it now. That girl who came to your house. Erma's friend. It's like she's standing right behind me."

I snatched the bag out of his hand and pulled him toward me.

"What are you—"

"Just hush and get over here," I hissed. "She *is* right behind you." I pointed toward the opening of the alcove. All I could see now was Erma's and Arthura's

hands as they played some sort of clapping and slapping game together. Chip dropped his remaining roller skate, and it bounced with a clang off the locker. Erma started to look over.

I had no choice. I grabbed Chip and pulled him into the corner in a hug. Erma looked harder. "What?" I heard Arthura say. Erma pointed into the alcove. I hugged Chip tighter and turned him so his back was to her. "Ew. Teenagers," Arthura said. She grabbed Erma's hand and they skated away.

I let out a breath and released Chip, who stumbled backward, his eyes watering. "That was a close one," he said.

"I know. I can't imagine what Erma would—"

"I knew it!" Erma said, popping around the corner, her

hands on her hips. "What are you two up to? Why are you hiding back here?"

"Shhh," I said. "Arthura will hear you."

Erma looked over her shoulder, then back at us, head cocked. "She's skating. Besides, what do you care if Arthura hears me, anyway? What are you hiding? What is that?" She was pointing at the bag, which was hanging limply at my side.

Chip and I looked at each other, and it wasn't lost on me that we were doing that Talking Without Talking thing that Samara and Dawson had done that day in the vestibule. He nodded, and I sighed. "Come in here." I scooted in tighter to make room for Erma. I handed her the bag. "This is what we're looking at."

"You're stealing chewed gum? That's pretty creepy, Thomas. I'm telling Mom that you're being creepy."

"I didn't steal it. I found it. *Arthura's* chewed gum. On the pedestal. Where the missing head used to sit. At my school." Erma looked at me like she still didn't get it, pinching the bag between two fingers like it was diseased. "Why would she be at my school, Erma? Why would she be around that pedestal?"

Erma shook her head and shrugged.

"It's admittedly circumstantial, but we believe it to be evidence of Arthura's presence at the scene of a crime. A larceny, to be exact."

Erma pointed to Chip. "You're weird."

He nodded. "I know."

"We think maybe Arthura is the one who stole the statue, Erma."

Erma laughed out loud. "Why would she want that old thing?"

"Why would I?" I countered. "But everyone seems to think I took it."

"Duh. To practice your magicky hoo-hoo on it." She wiggled her fingers in the air, the bag falling to the ground. I reached down and snatched it up. I finally had concrete evidence against someone, and I wasn't going to lose it now.

"So then what's your explanation for this?" I asked, wagging the bag at her.

She turned her palms up, frustrated. "Why don't you ask her?"

"Like she would tell us the truth," I said. "I need more evidence before I confront her." We all stood there, thinking. I had no idea how I was going to get more evidence from Arthura. She was not the most cooperative person in the world. And she definitely didn't trust me.

"Hey, I know! Will you help us get it?" Chip asked.

"No."

"Come on, Erma," I said. "This is important. Everyone hates me."

"Never."

"I'll teach you some magic."

She made a face. "I don't want to learn your dumb magic. I'm not five."

"I'll catch you your very own frog," Chip suggested.

"Disgusting."

I *thunk*ed my head against the locker a few times, and then it occurred to me. "I'll take your shift babysitting Grandma Jo next week. And I'll let you have my TV time."

She tapped her chin a few times, thinking about it, then leaned in. We both inched toward her. "Tell you what. I'll question her. I'll get it out of her without her even knowing it. Give me an hour, then meet me out back and I'll tell you what I found out." She pointed down the long corridor next to the rink. At the very end of the corridor—what was commonly known as Fifth-Grade Corner, on account of all the fifth graders who hung around back there—was a plain red metal door. Rumor was it was equipped with a silent alarm that went straight to the manager's office, and that only the baddest of the bad kids dared go through it. If you went through it, they said, the manager would handcuff you in his office and torture you. Or call the police. Or your parents, if they were scarier than the police.

I was pretty sure Mom was scarier than the police. Especially when she was on a Yelling at Thomas until Her Eyes Got Uneven and Her Vocal Cords Tied Themselves into Knots Adventure.

But Arthura was Erma's best friend. If there was anything to confide, Erma would get it out of her. It was a chance I had to take. I swallowed.

"Okay," I said. "We'll see you outside in an hour."

TRICK #23

WALKING THROUGH DOORS!

"You open it."

"No, you open it."

"You."

"You."

After Chip and I took off our skates, we spent a good majority of that hour trying to work up the nerve to open the back door. I had a feeling that the silent alarm and hand-cuffing manager were just stories. Rumors tended to go that way—just there to scare the heck out of kids like us. But I wasn't certain enough to want to give it a try. Because sometimes rumors worked.

"Come on, Chip, what's the worst thing that could happen? Just open it. We can pretend you fell into it. And hurry up—Erma won't ask Arthura until we leave."

"The worst thing that could happen is that I could end

up handcuffed in the manager's office. What if he never lets me out?"

Louis XIV: Handcuffed in skating rink manager's office for all eternity.

"Well, I can't be the one. I'm in enough trouble already with the missing head."

"Can't you do some of your magic and make it so we can just . . . walk through it?"

"I don't do that kind of magic, Chip. And no."

"Well, I'm not going to open it."

"Neither am I."

Erma skated by and gave us a death stare, a clueless Arthura skating by her side. *Get going,* Erma mouthed.

Chip and I both stared at the door, our arms crossed defiantly. I wished I could do some magic and just walk right on through, like Chip wanted. Grandpa Rudy would probably have been able to figure out a way to do it.

Chip turned to me. "Can we go out the front door and walk around to the back?"

I shook my head. "There's a fence." *And about a zillion teenagers who like to hang out by the side wall,* I didn't add. The truth was, teenagers kind of scared me, even when they weren't doing anything scary. The thought of pushing through a whole group of them around the side of a strange building made my heart pound practically out of my chest.

"What if we both opened it at the same time?" Chip

asked. "The rumor doesn't say anything about two sets of handcuffs. Only one. And they can't just blame one of us if both of us are guilty. They would be forced to let us go."

I gave him a stare. "They could handcuff us to each other." Which, when I thought about it, could be worse than being handcuffed by yourself in the manager's office.

I glanced at the skate floor. Erma was rounding the corner to come toward us again.

"Okay," I blurted. "Let's just give it a try."

We both placed our hands on the bar handle. We looked at each other and swallowed nervously. Chip's eyes were huge.

"You should see your eyes—they're huge," Chip said.

Okay, so apparently he wasn't the only one. "On three. One . . . two . . ."

And then right when I said "three" and shoved open the door, Chip pointed his finger in the air and said, "Are we pushing on three or are you going to say the word 'push' after th—"

"Really?" I asked, the door ajar, with my hands—and only my hands—all over it. "Are you kidding me?"

"What?"

"Nice," I said. "Way to leave me hanging, Chip."

"It's a common question in the rule of three," he said.

"It is not a common question. 'On three' means you push 'on three.' If I wanted to go on 'push,' I would have said, 'on push.'"

"Nobody says 'on push.'"

"Exactly!" I cried out, throwing my hands in the air. The door clanged shut. We both stared at it.

"Hurry up," I heard behind me, and turned just in time to see Erma whiz by again.

"You let the door shut," Chip said.

"Thank you. I know I let the door shut."

"What if the alarm is already sounding and the manager is getting out his handcuffs as we speak? We're going to have to reopen it. Are we going to do it on three or on pu—"

"Oh, here, just let me," I said, shoving open the door and slipping out, Chip trailing behind me.

The door shut with a soft click, snuffing out the music and lights on the other side as if they didn't even exist. My ears rang from the silence. It took my eyes a few seconds to adjust to the sunlight. Behind the rink there was a Dumpster that smelled like hot dogs, even from far away, and a Mr. Cheesy vending machine truck, its back door yawning open, exposing a dark interior.

"What do we do now?" Chip asked.

I shrugged. "We wait for Erma to show up, I guess." I leaned against the truck and crossed my legs, trying to look a thousand percent more casual than I felt. Chip bent to pick up pieces of gravel, which he held up to the light and squinted at, one by one. Time ticked by. It seemed like forever. It seemed so long that I wondered if Erma had gone home. All I had to measure by was the click of Chip's rocks hitting the ground, one by one. So far he'd dropped one hundred forty-two.

"Hey, Thomas?" Chip asked.

"Hmmm."

"Do you think she'll actually come out here?"

"You were right there. You heard her say she would."

"Yeah, but . . . I mean, won't she be afraid of the door, too?"

I thought about it. Erma was a lot of things, and most of them not good. She was pesky and loud and messy and sometimes downright annoying. And she lived to stick it to me. But would she go this far? Would she set me up to walk through the forbidden door at the skating rink and get trapped inside the fence . . . if I didn't get handcuffed by the manager in the process?

Yes. She totally would.

"It's a setup," I said angrily. "When I get my hands on Erma, I'm going to—"

But I didn't get to finish my sentence, because just then the door *clunk*ed and slowly opened. A man pressed through it, back-first.

The manager? Maybe. With handcuffs? Probably not. But I wasn't going to wait around to find out.

"Chip!" I whispered, "Follow me!"

I quickly assessed our situation. It was going to be either

hide inside the Dumpster or hide inside the truck. A swarm of flies created a black cloud over the Dumpster. The truck it was! I hopped up on my rear end and swiveled so I was facing what looked like dozens of boxes of vending machine snacks. Chip scrambled up next to me, our clothes making *shush* noises against the metal floor as we scooted backward on our rumps.

"In the back," I whispered.

On our hands and knees, we crawled to the back of the truck and wedged ourselves between a box of cheese puffs and a box of cheese-flavored tortilla chips. We held our breath, staying as still as humanly possible. Chip's leg rubbed up against mine.

But instead of an angry manager yelling at us to show ourselves, the man started whistling. The rattle of something metal rolling on the ground got louder and louder. I leaned forward and squinted between two boxes.

The man was wearing blue coveralls, a giant patch with the words Mr. Cheesy Makes Cheese Eesey ironed onto the back. He was pushing an empty metal trolley.

"Vending machine man," I whispered.

"Oh, no," Chip said. "He's going to be unloading these boxes. We're doomed."

"Shhh! We're not doomed yet. But we will be if you keep talking. When he goes back in with another load, we'll get out and climb the fence."

"But I'm not wearing my fence-climbing socks."

"Then you'll just have to wing it. Shhh."

Chip was silent, and we both listened as the whistling got closer until it was right in the open doorway. Then there was a grunt, and I watched as the Mr. Cheesy guy hefted the trolley into the back of the truck. And then before I could even stand up and say, "Wait!" he hopped up onto the bumper, reached for a cloth loop, and jumped down, pulling the truck door with him. It clattered shut.

"No, no," I said, trying to unfold myself from between the boxes. It was hard work now; the inside of the truck was so dark that it felt like it had weight. "No, no, no!" I fumbled for the door or a wall or . . . anything. I kept tripping over boxes and coming upon dead ends. "Let us out!"

But instead of the door opening and saving us, I heard another door thud behind me, and soon after, the truck rumbled to life. I lunged for the wall and started banging on it with both fists. "Help! Help! Chip, pound with me!"

There was a grinding of gears, and then the truck started moving, making me tumble back into my spot next to Chip. Trapped. I was trapped inside a chip truck with Chip Mason.

"Now what?" I asked. I kicked a box of cheesy whatevers in front of me. I turned on Chip. "You didn't even try to get them to hear us. You never said a word. You just sat here."

Next to me there was silence. And then some rustling. And then a crunch.

"You're eating? How can you be eating at a time like this?"

"Criminal activity apparently works up an appetite. Look on the bright side, Thomas," Chip said. "You're surrounded by all the cheese snacks you could imagine."

"I'm not hungry," I said.

"But it could help you with your history project," he countered. "It's a research trip!"

There was more crunching, and as we rolled along to who-knew-where, Chip loudly began slurping the excess cheese off his fingers. I secretly hoped it fused his mouth shut.

I leaned against the box next to me and closed my eyes, imagining Erma's delight at getting to tell Mom that I disappeared through the back door of the skating rink. Chip could look on the bright side all he wanted, but the truth was the truth.

We were trapped in this truck.

And I was going to be in so much trouble when I got out.

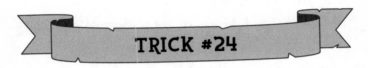

TRICK #24

I'LL NOW MAKE WATER APPEAR

By the time the truck rolled to a stop, I was pretty sure Chip was fast asleep next to me. Either that or my cheese-fused-mouth wish had come true, because, for a change, he wasn't talking.

I didn't know how he could sleep at a time like this. It was like nothing could rattle Chip Mason. He was what Grandma Jo would call "cool as a cucumber," whatever that meant. I would think a cucumber sitting out in a sunny garden would be hot. But I wasn't a gardener, so what did I know?

All I knew was there was no way I could have fallen asleep in the back of that truck. All I could think about was the many adventures I was going to have when I got out of here.

- The Mom's Head Actually Explodes This Time Adventure
- The Taking Away Everything but Your Mattress and a Glass of Lukewarm Water Adventure
- The Erma Is Now and Forever Known as the Good Child Adventure (gag)
- The You're Grounded Until They Invent JetPacks for School Buses Adventure

None of those adventures sounded good at all. Which was a real bummer, because I definitely wasn't having fun on the Trapped in a Cheesy Truck Adventure, either. If I was going to be subject to Mom's many adventures, I wanted to at least have had fun getting there.

I stood as soon as the truck stopped, nudged Chip awake with my toe, and felt my way to where I thought the door might be. When it roared open, I threw my hands up to block out the sun and yelped, staggering. The Mr. Cheesy man gasped and clutched his chest, also staggering.

"What the . . . ?" he kept saying over and over again. "What the . . . Where did . . . What the . . . ?"

"Hello, sir," I heard from behind me. "I believe I owe you recompense for your fine cheesy refreshment. I'm afraid, however, that I'm without capital at the moment. Will you take an IOU?"

I turned and glared at him. "Chip! Not now! You're not even wearing your vocabulary socks." And, no, I couldn't believe I uttered that sentence, either.

"What the . . . ?" the Mr. Cheesy guy was still saying. "How did you get in there?"

"At the skating rink," I said. I held my wrists out and lowered my head in defeat. "You can arrest us now. Just get it over with."

To my surprise, rather than be angry, the Mr. Cheesy man laughed. "Well, you sure scared the heck out of me, but I hardly think that's reason to arrest you. Come on out of there and we'll call your mothers."

I would almost have rather been arrested.

When Mom got to us (turned out we were in an office building all the way on the other side of town), her whole face was a straight line.

"Get in, Chip. Your mom is busy with your grandfather, so she asked me to bring you both home," was the only thing anyone said all the way until we pulled into our driveway and Chip got out of the car.

Then she turned the straight-line face directly at me.

"What on earth could possibly be your explanation?" she asked.

"Erma set us up," I said.

She tilted her head to one side. "You expect me to believe that your ten-year-old sister is responsible for you ending up halfway across town in the back of a vending-machine van?"

"Yes?"

She made a face that told me she clearly didn't believe it, even if it was true.

"Look, Mom, I'm really sorry, but I found some evidence that Chip and I needed to investigate, and we accidentally got trapped in the truck. We tried pounding, but he didn't hear us."

"Evidence? What kind of evidence?"

"I found something near the pedestal where Mrs. Heirmauser's statue used to be."

The straight line came back. "Thomas, you need to stay away from that statue altogether."

"It's not even there," I said. "I'm trying to solve the case."

She held out her hand to stop me and closed her eyes. "Honestly, I don't know what's gotten into you these days. First the statue, and now this. It's not enough that I have your grandmother to contend with. Did you know she's been doing parkour?"

I felt my face redden. Her eyebrows went up.

"You knew? And you didn't tell me?" She pulled her keys out of the ignition and opened her door. "I swear, it's like I don't even know you anymore, Thomas. You can go to your room to think about everything you've done. And don't come out until I tell you to."

2

There was a knock on my door about two hours later. Dad poked his head into my room while I was right in the middle of hard-core mope. I was lying on my bed cadaver-style, with arms and ankles crossed, staring at my ceiling until the bumps started to blend and move and my eyes started to water. I let the tears run down into my ears. Side bonus: if I looked like I was crying when Mom came to check on me, maybe she would feel bad and let me out.

"Hey, Thomas. Can I come in?"

I shrugged. He took that as a yes—which I was hoping he'd do, even if I couldn't say it out loud. He sat on the edge of the bed, facing away from me.

"I heard what happened," he said.

I said nothing. After a pause, he went on.

"Your mother says you tried to blame it on Erma?"

I shrugged.

"She's ten years old. You have to give her a break."

I rolled my eyes, thinking about poor, innocent, sweet, ten-year-old Erma and how it was completely unbelievable that she could do anything rotten. Boy, did she ever have my parents fooled. He shifted his weight, jiggling me, but I managed to keep myself all crossed up tight.

"Listen. You're probably going to need to apologize to your mom for worrying her today. And . . ."

He never finished the sentence. I could see him chewing on his lower lip a little, as if he was trying to figure out exactly how to say what he wanted to say.

"And what?" I asked, when I couldn't take it anymore.

"Well, if there's anything you need to talk about . . . anything you need to tell me—you know, anything you need to confess . . ."

I sat up. "Like what?"

This time it was his turn to shrug, only it didn't look nearly as casual as he wanted it to. "Oh, I don't know. If you got a bad grade on something or you're behind on your history project or, I don't know, if you have something you need to return."

"I've told you," I said. "I didn't steal the statue. I'm trying to find out who did steal it so I can get it back. That's how I got locked in the truck. But nobody believes me."

Dad patted my leg. "Sure, sure. I believe you. I do. But if you should change your mind and decide you did accidentally take something, you can come to me."

"How do you accidentally take a hundred-pound statue?"

He narrowed his eyes. "How do you know how much it weighs?"

I threw up my hands in despair. "I don't! I was guessing! I didn't take anything, accidentally or on purpose. I wish you believed me. I wish Mom believed me. I wish someone other than Chip Mason believed me."

"I believe you. I do, Thomas."

But for some reason, now *I* didn't believe *him*. Probably because he was still calling me "Thomas" instead of "pal." I flopped back onto my pillow with a grunt. He patted my leg again.

"So. Movie night? I've got *Attack of the Killer Koala-Droid*."

Oh, man. The *Killer Koala-Droid* was a classic. Dad and I had a thing, ever since I was old enough to cover my eyes in fear. Every week we popped in a ridiculous old horror movie—the kind where you could sometimes even see guys in the background working the monster puppet's strings—and popped popcorn and kicked the girls out of the basement. It was our "guy time." I loved it.

But that was before Dad stopped believing in me.

"I think I'll pass," I said to the ceiling.

"You sure? The koala has red lasers for eyes that melt buildings right down to the ground." He made a humming noise and used his fingers to simulate shooting lasers.

I flicked a glance at him and then looked away. "I'm sure. Just watch it without me."

He looked uncertain, maybe even a little stung. He stood up slowly, smoothing the bedding where he'd just been sitting. "Well, okay. But if you change your mind, you know where to find me."

"I won't change my mind," I said to the ceiling. "I wouldn't want to accidentally steal your time."

Dad didn't say anything; just went to the door. "I'll be downstairs," he said, before closing it behind him.

This time I didn't have to pretend the tears in my ears were from crying.

I SHALL NOW TURN MY SISTER INTO A HUMAN

I kept to myself for the rest of the weekend. I didn't even look outside to see if Chip Mason was doing his usual weird stuff, maybe wearing gymnastics socks or archaeology socks or dog-petting socks or whatever other socks he might have. I didn't care. I just wanted to be left alone.

Which wasn't so easy for Erma to do. She came into my room Sunday morning, just as I was getting ready to give up and go down to the kitchen for some breakfast. I wanted to prove a point. But not as much as I wanted French toast.

"Hey," she said. She seemed sheepish.

"What do you want?" I snapped.

"To say I'm sorry." She was twisting the hem of her pajama shirt around in one palm. She was still in her pajamas but was wearing pink lip gloss. I could smell the strawberry all the way across the room. More proof that girls didn't understand life at all.

"You said it. Now get out," I said. I pretended to be really busy fixing the hinge on my magic case, even though it wasn't broken.

"Don't you even want to know what I found out?"

"No."

"After all that, you don't want to know whether or not Arthura did it? I would think you would at least want to make it worth your while. You're not even curious?"

Yes. Of course I was. I was dying to know what Erma found out about Arthura. But I didn't want to give Erma the pleasure of being the one to tell me anything.

But she was the only one who knew.

I sighed. "What did you find out about Arthura?"

She came in and shut the door. Walked over to my bed and sat on her knees. Leaned in like she had a huge secret. Despite trying to act cool, I found myself absently winding my never-ending handkerchief around my hand again and again while leaning toward her. It got very quiet in my room.

"She didn't do it," she said.

"That's it? She didn't do it?"

She turned her palms up. "She didn't do it."

"How do you know?"

"Because she told me."

I tossed the hanky back into the case, only it was so

wrapped around my hand that it didn't go anywhere. I tried to quickly unwrap it, but it's basically impossible to look cool quickly undoing something that's all knotted up around a body part. Especially a never-ending something. "Of course she said she didn't do it. Did you think she was going to confess?"

Erma scrunched up her nose and lips, thinking. "Yeah. She would tell me."

"No way."

"Yes way."

"No way, Erma."

She stood and placed her fists on her hips. "Yes way, Thomas. Besides, she told me how the gum got there."

"You asked?"

"I told you I would."

"You also set me up to be stuck in a vending-machine supply truck."

"I only set you up to be locked outside," she said, holding up one finger. "I didn't know about the truck. I was going to let you back in eventually."

I glared at her. Her shoulders drooped.

"I'm sorry, Thomas, okay?"

I paused, staring at her long enough to make her feel squiggly inside but not so long that she would walk out and take her Arthura story with her. "Okay," I said. "Now spill."

"So, it turns out that Arthura's aunt Mandy is a police

officer. And she was the one who came when the school called about the missing statue. According to Arthura, her aunt Mandy had borrowed a piece of gum from Arthura that morning and was chewing it when she went on the call. And apparently when she bent down to look for evidence, someone opened the front door and a big gust of wind blew in and blew the dust right off the pedestal and into Mandy's face. She sneezed out her gum. She couldn't find it—she looked everywhere—but it was gone. That's how the gum got there. It was never Arthura's to begin with."

"That's a dumb story."

"It is not!"

"Yes, it is. It's a dumb story."

Erma's fists went right back to her hips. She must have had fist-shaped dents permanently imprinted in her skin. "You're a dumb story!"

"That doesn't make any sense. And neither does your story. That gum was covered with glittery lip gloss. Just like Arthura wears."

"And like her aunt wears, too," she said. "Police officers can wear lip gloss, you know."

I didn't know if that was true or not, but I knew my sister, and even though the story was pretty dumb, she totally believed it. And if she believed it, maybe it would be worth my while to believe it, too. Besides, why *would* Arthura want the statue? I still had no answer for that.

"Thanks," I said. "For nothing."

"You're welcome," she said, pointing her nose up to the ceiling. "And just so you know, Arthura said she wouldn't be surprised if her aunt Mandy came to talk to you about the case pretty soon."

"Sure, sure," I said. "Arthura is so reliable." I rooted around in the magic case for Grandpa Rudy's old bottle of sulfur hexafluoride. I felt like making something float.

"Hey, Thomas?" Erma said.

I didn't even look up. "What?"

"I'm sorry that Arthura wasn't the one. But just so you know, I don't think you did it, either."

She skipped out of the room before I could absorb what she said. I looked up just in time to see her pigtails bouncing through my doorway. Someone besides Chip believed me.

It was Erma, but Erma was someone.

Maybe she didn't have my parents so fooled after all.

Just then I heard a commotion outside. I pulled up on my knees and peered out my window. Chip Mason, wearing a helmet and knee pads that reminded me a lot of Grandma Jo's parkour gear, was inside a metal trash can, rolling down his driveway and crashing to a stop against our mailbox. Then he got up, dragged the trash can back to the top of his driveway, climbed inside, and did it all over again.

I shook my head.

Erma may have believed me, but that didn't change the

facts. The head was still missing. Everyone thought I stole it. Now a lip gloss–wearing police officer was going to question me.

And we still had no idea who the real thief was.

TRICK #26

ALACAZAM! A PLAN!

On Monday morning, I awoke to the sound of something tapping against my window. I flew out of bed and grabbed my straw, expecting another snowstorm of spitwads. But when I flung back the curtain, straw poised in my mouth, I found Chip Mason standing on the other side, waving at me excitedly.

He was still wearing his pajamas, which were basically a big, furry teddy bear suit. Complete with a hood with ears.

Who wants to start their morning talking to an eighty-pound teddy bear with freckles? Not me, but I opened the window anyway.

"Good morning, Thomas!" Chip said, leaning so far through my window that he was practically in my room. "What are you doing on this fine day?"

"I was asleep. Like a normal person," I said. As if on cue,

my alarm clock buzzed. Time to get up for school. Dread. I slapped it into snooze and turned back to Chip. "What do you want?"

"I saw something," he said excitedly. Knowing Chip, it was an especially bright firefly, or maybe a documentary about bricks.

"Good for you," I said. "I have to take a shower now." I started to close the window, but he refused to move out of the way.

"I saw it on Saturday night," he said. "After . . . you know."

Yeah, I knew. After Mom's Straight Line for a Face Adventure.

"I've been dying to tell you about it, but you never came out of your house."

"I'm sort of grounded forever," I said, which wasn't true. Unless you count that I'd pretty much grounded myself.

"Huh," he said. "My mom made me write an essay about my adventure so she could put it in my baby book."

It didn't sound like Chip's mom had the same idea about adventures as mine did. And Chip was still putting things in a baby book?

"Don't you want to know what I saw?" he prodded.

I closed my eyes and counted to five. "Okay, Chip, what exactly did you see?"

He spread out his hands dramatically. "It was the dark of night. The clock had struck seven. Owls were hooting, crickets were chirping, the moon was a waning gibbous. Or was it a waxing gibbous? You know, I always tend to get those mixed up. Which is really odd, since at fourth-grade space camp, this kid—his name was Arcturus, by the way, which is a funny name, but you see, he was named after the—"

"Chip!" I practically yelled, then remembered that it was early morning and lowered my voice. "Would you just get to what you saw already? I have to go to school. And won't your bus be here soon?"

"I'm getting to that," he said. "And don't remind me."

So, obviously things still weren't going well for Chip at Boone Public. I couldn't explain why, but this kind of made me angry, like I needed to go over to Brandon's house and tell him that there was Avoiding the New Kid, and then there was just plain mean.

I motioned for him to continue. "Well, get to it. Fast forward past fourth-grade space camp. And fifth-grade space camp, too. And any other camps that might pop into your head."

He nodded. "Okay. Well, my grandpa was having a really bad craving for ice cream. But not just any ice cream. He wanted ice cream from Cathy's Cow Barn. Butter brickle double chocolate chip. His favorite flavor."

Cathy's Cow Barn was in town and was practically a monument in Boone County. It had been around . . . well, about as long as Helen Heirmauser had been. It was pretty much the only place anyone ever went to get ice cream.

"And?" I nudged. "I want to know this why?"

"And so my mom and I went to Cathy's Cow Barn to get my grandpa some ice cream, because he's not doing very well, and Mom says when a guy who feels like Grandpa feels wants some butter brickle, then he should get some butter brickle, even if it's a pain for the people having to get it for him."

I was annoyed that Chip still hadn't gotten to his point, but his face flushed pink when he talked about his grandpa, and it didn't seem like the right time to hassle him about one of his stories.

"Anyway. So we were driving to Cathy's Cow Barn, and I saw a kid. He was wearing a black hoodie and one of those flimsy string backpacks and going into a building." He leaned in and whispered, "An abandoned building." He raised and lowered his eyebrows a few times like he'd just said something really important.

"I don't get it," I said. "So?"

"So he kept looking over his shoulder as he was going into the building, like he was trying not to be seen. He walked around the street lamps, in the shadows with the hooting owls and the chirping crickets, where even a full moon couldn't get to him, had it been a full moon, which it definitely was not. I know that much for sure."

"What are you trying to tell me, Chip?"

"His backpack," he said. "It sagged down almost to the backs of his knees. It looked heavy." He darted a glance over his own shoulder, then leaned in again. "And it was head shaped."

"Are you sure?" I whispered. "Like, one hundred percent?"

He nodded excitedly. "He went into the building, but first, he took off his hoodie. And you know what was underneath?" I shook my head, transfixed by Chip's story now. "A brown vest and bow tie."

"He's from—"

"Pennybaker School," Chip finished for me.

"What did he look like? What color was his hair?"

Chip shook his head sadly. "It was dark, and Mom was hurrying to get to Cathy's before it closed. I didn't have time for details."

Except for hooting owls and chirping crickets and a waxing gibbous moon, but I didn't point that out. "That's okay," I said. "You remember where this building is?"

"Yep." He tapped his temple. "Got it memorized. You wanna go there after school? We can ride our bikes."

"Definitely. Maybe we can figure out who this kid is and find the statue, and then I'll be off the hook."

7

I could barely concentrate on anything at school. I didn't even care when Buckley and Colton swapped my desk with the uneven one again. I *thunk*ed my way through Facts After the Fact class without even realizing, my mind solely on who could have been the mystery kid with the head-shaped backpack. I watched everyone closely for signs.

I was so certain that Chip and I had the thief that I didn't even notice that Patrice Pillow was hanging out in the restroom hallway by the science-floor greenhouse until she tripped me when I walked by. I sprawled across the floor, my books flying out of my hands and the last button popping off my vest and plunging off the balcony.

"What the—?" I said, pulling myself up and rubbing my elbow, which I'd bumped on the tile.

"Shhh! Just come here," Patrice said. "Hurry up."

There were monsters doodled all over the bottom of the notebook Patrice cradled in her arms. I was starting to think Patrice Pillow, while she seemed nice, was someone I wouldn't want to run into outside of an abandoned warehouse with the hooting owls and the chirping crickets. I hoped she wasn't the kid Chip had seen.

She pulled my elbow, leading me into the hallway. "Are you going to write me into a story and kill me?" I asked.

"Already have," she said. "That's not what I want. I just wanted to tell you something. The plans you saw about the spitwad war? The ones on Flea's computer? It's not the original boy versus girl war. It's an everybody versus Thomas war. You need to watch your back. Just in case they decide to ambush you."

"Ambush?" I asked. "Everyone against me?" My hand automatically went to my pocket, but I remembered too late that in all my excitement over what Chip had seen, I'd accidentally left my straw at home. My heart skipped a beat. I felt a coating of sweat cover my upper lip. I rubbed it away. "When?"

"I'm not sure about the details. All I know is I heard Wesley and Flea talking to Samara and AnneMarie, the leaders of the girls' side. I heard your name, and I heard the word 'ambush,' and I saw them high-five each other. There is no way Samara would high-five the leader of the boys' side unless they were planning something together."

Wesley. Of course. I knew somebody had to be organizing the snowstorm on my window.

"Okay," I said. "Thanks for letting me know. I'll watch out for them."

"No problem," she said. She picked at the stray paper

bits in the spiral of her notebook, staring down as if she was nervous about something. Probably about being caught tipping me off. "Just be careful."

"I will." I started to walk out of the hallway, then changed my mind and turned back. "Hey, Patrice?"

She looked up from her notebook. "Yeah?"

"Why are you helping me?" I asked.

She smiled. "Because I think I was wrong," she said. "I don't think you're the cat."

I couldn't change into my shorts and T-shirt fast enough. The sun would be going down before too long, Cathy's Cow Barn was pretty far away, and Mom didn't like me to be out on my bike after dark. We were going to have to ride fast.

The ride to Cathy's is flat and tree lined, and we took mostly side streets so we could avoid cars. The air was warm and the sky sunny, and Chip and I took turns doing stunts like riding with no hands and standing on our pedals and lifting one leg and even closing our eyes for a few seconds. We didn't talk about the statue or the spitwad war or our mission to catch the real thief. For a second, I forgot that everything was falling apart and that Chip was completely insane. For a second, I felt like I was just riding my bike on a nice day with a friend. Which was something I hadn't done in forever.

When we got downtown, we moved over to the sidewalk. Not that there were a ton of cars in the downtown stretch of Boone City, but there were definitely more than we were used to, and Chip was getting pretty tired from pedaling.

We got to Cathy's Cow Barn and left our bikes against the wall. We went inside, where Chip sprang for vanilla ice cream for both of us. We sat on the sidewalk in front of our bikes and ate them while the sun began to sink. I knew we needed to get moving, but I figured it was probably a smart move for us to get some energy before the long ride back.

Besides, we were playing a pretty fun game of I spy. Chip was terrible at it. He liked details. And a guy who likes details gives away way too many clues in I spy.

"I spy with my little eye . . . something red. And blue. With a basketball on the front of it. And the words 'Nuttin but Net.' Spelled incorrectly, I might point out. And it's made out of a polyester-cotton blend. Size youth extra-large. With a new ice cream stain on the sleeve."

"Chip. That's my shirt. You have to get less specific."

"Okay. I spy with my little eye . . . a car."

"Better."

"With the license plate UNI 987."

"Not better."

We played until we were out of ice cream and out of things to spy.

"The building is around the corner there," Chip said when we'd finished. He clipped his helmet back on and pointed toward a deserted area of town. "Follow me."

As we got closer to the warehouse, my throat dried up and my stomach started to get tingly, like when I knew I was in trouble and Dad was about to go mushroom cloud on me.

Louis XIV: Hit by a mushroom cloud of Dad doom.

"Hey, Chip," I panted. He seemed to be getting faster and faster. "Maybe we shouldn't be doing this."

He slowed to a stop. "It's that building there," he said.

Too late. We were already doing this.

The building was enormous—a gray concrete-block rectangle that seemed to go on forever. The roof was metal and wavy and rusted. The windows—the ones that didn't have rock holes in them—were filthy and covered with boards. In the center of the wall we were facing, there was a set of double doors, coated with peeling paint.

"What do you suppose this building was used for?" I asked.

Chip removed his helmet again. "Maybe some sort of roofing-supply company? Or car parts or something?"

"Or it was a meat factory owned by a crazy man with saws for hands. Meat Man." We blinked at each other. Clearly, I needed to stop talking to Patrice Pillow. "Sorry. So now what do we do?"

"We see if we can look in one of those windows." He stepped off his bike, rolled it a few feet, and leaned it against a Dumpster. He acted like he'd done this a million times. Like it wasn't terrifying at all. I was forced to wheel my bike next to his or look like a wimp. There was no way I was going to look like a wimp compared to Chip Mason. The guy wore fluffy bunny slippers. Pink ones.

"So, I was just thinking," I said as we walked to the building. Our feet were moving way too fast for my taste. "What if there's a whole stolen-art ring going on, and this place is patrolled by the mob or something?" I could almost hear Wesley's mafia voice in my head. It made me miss him a little. Until I reminded myself that he was the ringleader of an ambush with my name on it.

"I don't know," Chip said. "I guess we'll figure it out when we get there."

"But what if they grab us and tie us up and put blindfolds over our eyes and potatoes in our mouths?"

"And you say I have an overactive imagination," Chip said. "Just relax and see if you can see through that window."

I craned my neck. The windows were a lot higher than they looked from across the street. "How am I supposed to get up there?"

Chip thought about it, chewing on his lip. "You could stand on my shoulders."

I remembered how much his feet dug into my palms when I boosted him in through the window at Pennybaker. There was no way he would be able to handle my shoes digging into his shoulders.

It would hurt.

Payback.

"Okay."

He hooked his hands together and bent low. I put my foot in his hands, but just as I was about to put my full weight on him, there was a noise behind us. A noise like footsteps and someone humming.

"Did you hear that?" I whispered.

Chip nodded.

"What is it?"

"I don't know," Chip said, and then his eyes grew wide as he spotted something over my shoulder. "Quick! Hide!"

We raced behind a stack of old pallets and hunkered down. I watched through the pallet slats as a kid in a hoodie walked toward the double doors. He was wearing a string backpack. A head-shaped string backpack. He looked over his shoulders, once, twice, let his backpack slide to the ground, and then took off his hoodie. Underneath were a brown vest and bow tie. And he was holding a long, skinny balloon.

A balloon-animal balloon.

The thief was Harvey Hinkle.

I rubbed my eyes and looked again. Sure enough, there was the curly red hair, the thin arms, and the balloon that I knew so well from Facts After the Fact class.

Harvey Hinkle ducked into the building, and the doors slammed closed behind him. Chip and I came out from behind the pallets.

"Well?" Chip said proudly. "Did I tell you, or did I tell you?"

"I know that kid," I said angrily. "He's in my history class."

"And he has a head in that backpack. And unless it's a human head—doubtful, by the way, as a human head that's not attached to a human body tends to smell pretty bad and . . . leak things—it has to be our missing head."

"That thief. That liar. That . . . that . . ."

"Bandit? Crook. Plunderer!" Chip shook his fist while he said the last, then looked at my face and lowered his arm dejectedly. "I know. No vocabulary socks."

I decided to let it go. I was too mad at Harvey Hinkle to be annoyed at Chip. "We have to get it back."

"Yes."

I paced back and forth in front of the pallets. "But we don't know what's inside the building. It could be dangerous in there."

"True."

I paced some more. "But if we catch Harvey Hinkle red-handed, then the world will have no choice but to believe my innocence."

"Correct."

"So let's go!" I started for the door, but Chip held me back.

"We can't."

"Why not?"

This time it was his turn to pace. "These sorts of things have to be handled delicately. With finesse. We can't just walk in with no plan. We have no camera. No recording device. It would be our word versus his."

"You're right," I said. "We need a plan." I felt like

someone in a spy movie, like I should be wearing a tuxedo or something.

"Plus, it's getting dark, and our moms are going to be mad at us."

I stared at him. This was definitely not a cool time to bring up a guy's mom. Even if Chip was right.

Chip went back to pacing. "Let's go home and plan a reverse heist. You tail Harvey Hinkle at school, and I'll tail him after he gets home. And then we'll come back here tomorrow night and take back the statue and get proof that Harvey was the one who stole it."

We hopped on our bikes and headed home, talking the whole while. By the time we got home, we had a plan.

We were going to steal back the statue.

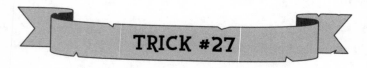

TRICK #27

DISAPPEARING FROM SCHOOL

The next morning, Principal Rooster was waiting for me in the vestibule. As usual, several students were congregating around the empty pedestal, talking in hushed voices, but most of them were looking at me from the moment I walked in the door. I had been thinking about Harvey Hinkle and how Chip and I were going to surprise him tonight and get the statue back, but even I could feel the tension in the air. I slowed, and then recovered, heading straight for my first class.

"Mr. Fallgrout," Principal Rooster said as I tried to slip by. He stepped into my path.

"Yes, sir?" I squeezed my arms tighter around my books, hoping to conceal my vest, which had a way of flopping like a cape when I walked fast, now that it had no buttons.

"I'm wondering if I can have a moment," he said. He

stepped to the side and held his arm out so that it was pointing toward his office. I knew that meant he wasn't really wondering; he was just trying to be polite about telling me to get into his office, pronto.

I followed him past Miss Munch, who glanced up at me and then pointed her face straight down at her keyboard. She even used one hand to shield her eyes, though she tried to make it look like she was just holding her forehead in her hand.

Principal Rooster paused in his doorway and again used the arm-gesture thing. I wondered what he would do if I said, "Oh, no, no. That's okay. I think I'll pass." Which was totally what I wanted to do. But then I was pretty sure I knew the outcome of that, and Mom would definitely not appreciate a Thomas Is Suspended for Being Flip Adventure.

After I sat, Principal Rooster shut the door and pulled down the blinds, so that it got murky in his office. He reached over me and turned on a lamp. It lit up the room in a way that felt weird—like I was in his living room instead of his office. He took his time walking around his desk and sitting down in his big, cushiony chair, then he leaned forward and laced his hands together. He wasn't wearing his usual good-natured grin. His eyes weren't sparkling. His cheeks weren't pushing up toward his eyes. I didn't think it was possible, but he looked . . . mad.

I gulped. "Is something wrong?" I asked in a teeny-tiny voice that Erma would have loved to have heard come out of my mouth.

Principal Rooster stared at his fingers. "Well, yes, of course something is wrong, Mr. Fallgrout. Something is very wrong." He looked up at me with his not-Principal-Rooster eyes, and I shrank back.

"Y-you mean the statue?" I asked.

"Yes, of course I mean the statue. I think it's time we talked." His voice was still very measured. Icy. He picked up a paperclip and turned it in his fingers. "Do you know who Helen Heirmauser was, Thomas?"

"A math teacher?" I ventured.

He nodded. "Yes, she was a math teacher, but she was more than that, Thomas. You see, Helen Heirmauser was a math *genius*. She could remember what day of the week it was on any given date in her lifetime. She could multiply ten-digit numbers in her head if she wanted. Have you ever heard of pi, Thomas?"

I licked my lips nervously. "Like . . . the food?"

"No, like the number. Do you know how many digits are in pi, Thomas?"

"No."

"Trillions. More than trillions. It's infinite, Thomas, and it's also not a rational number, so the digits don't repeat."

"Okay," I said uncertainly.

He stood and paced to a bookshelf, then picked up a globe paperweight and held it in his hand. "Helen Heirmauser had pi memorized to more than eighty thousand digits. Eighty thousand, Thomas! Until 2006, she was the world record holder. Right here in our very school. That's more than just a math teacher, wouldn't you agree?" He tossed the paperweight in his hand a few times.

I nodded, just in case he had plans to chuck it at me. Weirder things had happened lately.

"But there was more to it. Helen Heirmauser was the first truly uniquely gifted individual at Pennybaker School, after Louis Pennybaker himself. And she embraced it. Do you know what happens to most kids who are uniquely gifted, Thomas?"

"No, sir."

"They aren't accepted. They're thought of as weird. Unusual. Dorky."

I thought about my magic and how I didn't talk about it at my old school. How I kept the trunk in my room, most of the time under my bed, and still considered it something just between me and Grandpa Rudy. I thought about how embarrassed I was to admit that I was good at magic to pretty much anyone. It was sort of like having a dirty little secret. Even though there was nothing wrong with it, and, in fact, being really good at something unique was actually pretty cool.

Principal Rooster put the paperweight back on the shelf, then came over and sat on the edge of his desk, towering over me. "Helen Heirmauser accepted everyone's gifts. It was her passion. It was her calling. It is the reason our students, and the students before them and the students all the way back to your grandparents' generation and maybe even beyond, hold her in such high regard. She earned it, one accepting hug at a time. Do you understand what I'm getting at, Thomas?"

"That's why everyone's so upset that the statue is missing?"

"Stolen. Not missing—stolen." He got up and went back to his chair. "And maybe it was stolen by someone who didn't quite understand its importance. Someone who maybe went to a different school before this year. Someone who maybe understands things now and might want to return it?"

He stared at me so intently that I started to feel myself squirm. "But I didn't take it, sir."

He closed his eyes, as if the words physically hurt him.

"We both know that isn't true, Mr. Fallgrout."

"But it *is* true. I had nothing to do with it. I'm trying to find it, too. I want it to come back so people will talk to me again."

"The longer you keep it, the less likely that is to happen, you know."

"But I don't have it!"

He stared at me a few moments longer, as if he could stare a confession out of me. Then he took a deep breath and leaned back in his chair. He picked up his phone and said, "Miss Munch? Would you mind getting Thomas Fallgrout's parents on the phone?" He hung up. "I didn't want to do this, but I'm afraid you leave me no choice. Your straw, please." He stretched a hand, palm-up, across his desk.

At first I didn't know what he was talking about. And then I realized he meant my special team captain straw. My *secret* special team captain straw for the *secret* spitwad war that nobody was supposed to know about. "I don't know what you're talking—"

He wiggled his fingers. "Hand it over, please."

With shaky hands, I dug it out of my pocket and placed it in his palm. Now I was unarmed. A terrifying feeling, given what Patrice had told me. "But there's an ambush coming," I said softly.

"I'm afraid you're going to be suspended for instigating a schoolwide spitball fight, Mr. Fallgrout. Yes, we know all about the spitwad fight. Nurse Hale is preparing a lecture on the dangers of germ-soaked weaponry as we speak."

"But I didn't instigate it."

"Wesley tells us you're the leader of the boys' team."

That stinkball Wesley. He double-crossed me. First he kicked me out of the leader position, and then he turned me in for being the leader. "I'm not anymore. Nobody will even talk to me. They spitwadded my window. At my house."

"Nobody reported anything," Principal Rooster said. He slid open a drawer and dropped my straw into it. Then he laced his hands together. "Hopefully the time off will give you a chance to think, Mr. Fallgrout. Some time to reflect about things."

I was so mad I was shaking. Worse, there were tears bubbling up in my eyes. I couldn't say anything. It seemed pointless to even try.

Principal Rooster stood and went to the door. He opened it and stood to one side. "You can wait outside for your mother to get here."

Great.

TRICK #28

FLOATING TO CATHY'S COW BARN

"You ready to go?" Chip said that evening, showing up at my window again. I wondered if Chip knew doors existed. He was already wearing his pads and helmet. And a very long pair of gray socks that went all the way up to where his shorts ended. He saw me staring. "My sneaking socks," he said. "I'm quiet as a mouse in these."

I had a hard time imagining Chip being as quiet as an anything, ever.

"So, you ready?" he asked again. "The sun's going down soon."

"I'm not sure," I said. "I think I might be grounded."

Not true. Mom didn't even yell when she picked me up from school. Her face wasn't a straight line, either. Instead it kind of drooped down into a whole-face frown. Her voice sounded kind of strange and watery when she talked to Miss

Munch, and when she came out of Principal Rooster's office, her eyes looked red, too.

I had made my mom cry. I was the worst son ever.

But then I reminded myself that I didn't actually do anything wrong.

When we got home, I went straight to my room and was afraid to come out again. Maybe not ever again. Maybe they would slip my food in through the crack under the door and I would make my own clothes out of my bedspread and wouldn't shave and would turn wild. Maybe I would forget how to talk to humans, and when they finally came to get me out, I would swat at them with my animal claws, lice and rats and stuff flinging out of my matted hair.

"Wouldn't you know if you're grounded?" Chip asked. A reasonable question.

"They're kind of not talking to me. But I got suspended today, so I'm guessing Mom wouldn't be too excited to let me go out tonight."

"But we have plans," Chip said. "I'm wearing my sneaking socks and everything."

"Sorry."

"Okay." He turned and moped away from the window. But before I could close it, he came back. He held one finger up in the air—a pose I knew meant he had an idea. "But, you see, if we're successful tonight—and I've run the algorithms; our prospects are good—we will have the proof that you are wrongly accused. Your innocence will be irrefutable. They'll have no choice but to apologize to you. Maybe even make a bust out of your head and put it right next to hers. Parades, Thomas—they might have parades for you. A hero's welcome." He lowered his chin and looked at me, all serious. "Thomas, you can't stay suspended forever. You can't stay the school pariah forever. And you can't just sit around and wait for the police to come ransack your room."

I didn't know what a pariah was, and I doubted all that about the parades, but he was right about one thing. If I managed to return the statue, I would be out of trouble and my life could go back to normal. Well, to what normal had become, anyway.

"You're right," I said. "Give me five minutes."

I lucked out. Mom was too busy trying to figure out where Grandma Jo had gone to worry about whether or not I should be allowed out of the house for the rest of my natural-born life. When I told her I was going on a bike ride with Chip, and that we would be home a little after dark, she gave me a distracted wave and continued trying to reach Grandma on her cell phone.

"Goodness only knows, the woman is cliff diving or snowboarding or . . . or . . . or testing explosives," she muttered to Dad.

"Hey, pal, we need to have a discussion, don't you think?" he called as I raced to the garage.

"We will, Dad, I promise." He started to say something else, but I interrupted. "This bike ride is important, Dad. You have to trust me on this."

He considered it, examining me, and then nodded. "Go ahead. We'll talk later."

I could hear Erma start to protest how "unfaaair" it was that I got to go outside and "plaaay" when I was so "baaad," but I shut her out with a slam of the garage door.

Chip was mounted and waiting for me on the street, bent over and fussing with his socks. Sneaking socks. How could he believe in such thing? Also, I hoped they worked.

As we rode, Chip told me the plan.

"We're going to hide our bikes behind Cathy's Cow Barn and walk," he said.

"Uh-huh."

"And then we're going to hide behind the pallets like we did last time, and wait for Harvey to get there."

"Okay."

"And we'll wait for him to go inside, and then grab the door and slip in behind him."

"Yeah?"

"And that's all I have."

I coasted so he could catch up. "That's it?"

"I had a geometry test," he said. "And Grandpa Huck was doing really bad today."

"Oh." I started pedaling again, so he didn't have to have me looking at him, just in case he wanted to start crying about his grandpa or something.

"Anyway, so I was thinking, once we have the head, we're probably going to have to call someone to help us out. It's forty-point-two pounds and one foot three inches by two feet exactly, and other than a small indentation where her mouth is, there really isn't anywhere to hang on to, especially if you take into consideration her slippery forehead. It would be very difficult to navigate our bikes while holding her. Plus, we wouldn't want to risk dropping her and damaging her."

"We could stop by Cathy's when we get our bikes and ask to use their phone. I'm sure my dad would come pick us up once he heard what we had." I got lost in a daydream about Dad patting me on the back and telling me I'd made him prouder than Erma ever could. And that they were wrong—my unique gift was actually solving crimes instead of magic.

Neither one of us had any money, which was too bad, because Cathy's vanilla cones were excellent. But my stomach was all knotty anyway, and I was sweating and panting from riding so fast. Also, a bug had flown in my mouth about a block earlier, and my gagger was still feeling kind of sensitive about it. What if the bug was still alive and ate the ice cream and got bigger and kept eating and getting bigger and eating and getting bigger while I was starving and getting smaller and smaller until one day all that was left was a giant talking bug pulling rabbits out of hats?

Louis XIV: Stuffed in a hat for all eternity by human-beetle hybrid magician.

We parked our bikes behind Cathy's and walked to the pallets and waited for Harvey Hinkle. I wished I'd gotten to see him at school that day. I wished I'd been able to tail him and report to Chip his every move, even down to what he had for lunch and how he held his fork.

Still, I knew the form I saw coming down the road was Harvey Hinkle even without tailing him. I could tell by the way the hoodie drooped over his head and the way his shoulders sagged from the weight of his backpack.

"There he is," I whispered.

"Wait," Chip said. "Just wait."

We watched as Harvey approached the door. I started to get up, but Chip pulled me back down by my sleeve.

"Wait for it, Thomas."

Harvey pulled open the door.

"Wait for what? He's getting away."

"Wait . . . wait . . ."

Harvey stepped through the door. I tried to tear Chip's fingers away from my clothes.

"Just a little . . . bit . . . longer . . ."

"It's going to be too late," I said. "Let go."

The door started to close behind Harvey.

"Now!" Chip yelled, and he was halfway to the door before I'd even gotten all the way out from behind the pallets.

Chip grabbed the door with only an inch to spare, ripped it open, scrambled through, and yelled, "Stop right there, Harvey Hinkle, you thief! We've caught you red—"

I practically bowled him over—I was running full tilt, and he'd stopped in his tracks. It took me a second to understand why. I gazed into the room beyond the door.

"What the . . . ?"

Harvey Hinkle dropped his backpack.

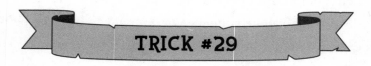

TRICK #29

IMPALED IN A BARREL

The first thing I noticed was the smell. Cow. To be precise, the stuff that comes out of a cow. And dirt, lots of dirt. We were standing on a dirt floor, which was lit up with lots of overhead lights and led to a walled-off ring. In the center of the ring was a brightly painted barrel. I heard a moo.

Harvey Hinkle was standing in front of us, his backpack on the ground between his feet, his hands in the air, surrender-style.

"What is this?" I asked. "Where are the mobsters?"

"Thomas Fallgrout?" Harvey said. "What are you doing here? What mobsters?"

"We're here to get back what's rightfully ours," Chip sneered. He reached down to grab the backpack.

I leaned toward him. "Technically, it's not ours. It belongs to the school, but yeah."

Chip had whipped the backpack off the ground so easily that there was no way it weighed forty-point-two pounds. Still, he reached inside triumphantly. "Harvey Hinkle," he intoned in an important voice, "we are charging you with burglary."

"Who's charging me?" Harvey asked. He'd let his hands down, and made a feeble swipe for the bag. "And what did I steal?"

I shrugged. "Never mind what he says. Just, we're here to get the head back so everyone will stop hating me."

"Why would you want the head?" Harvey Hinkle asked in a very confused voice.

"Because Helen Heirmauser was a genius and blah-blah-blah. I mean, I don't want the creepy thing. I just want to clear my name, okay?"

"Uh, Thomas?" Chip said. His arm was in the bag up to his elbow, and he had a funny look on his face.

"Quit with the theatrics, Chip. Let's just take the head and go."

"But that's the thing," Chip said.

"What does the head have to do with Helen Heirmauser?" Harvey Hinkle asked. He made another grab for the bag. "Give that to me. You'll tangle it."

Tangle it?

Tangle it?

How could someone tangle a bronze bust?

"Chip," I said warily. "What's in the bag?" Although I knew the answer wasn't going to be good from the look on his face.

"It's a head," Chip said, slowly pulling something bright red and curly out of the bag. It was a wig, attached to a Styrofoam head.

"That's not—" I started, but I couldn't finish due to the foghorn that was coming at me from the side.

"You two must be new students," the foghorn said, only it sounded like "YOU TWO MUST BE NEW STUDENTS!" with a thousand exclamation points after it.

The foghorn was coming out of a clown. A real, bona fide, rainbow-wig-wearing, white-makeup-with-big-red-lips-wearing, poofy-green-polka-dotted-suit-wearing clown.

Suddenly the head in Chip's hand made sense. Harvey Hinkle didn't steal the Heirmauser statue; he was carrying around a clown wig.

"No, we're—" Chip started, but the foghorn had engulfed him, clasping arms around each of our shoulders and leading us across the dirt floor to a makeup and dressing area on one end of the building.

"We're always so glad to have new students. Not enough young ones these days, you know? I mean, Harvey here is a real treat. A real treat, aren't you, Harvey? But he's my only young clown. My balloon-animal clown. We need more shapes and sizes. And you two are perfect. I have just the outfits for you. Come with me, come with me. Oh, I suppose I should introduce myself. I'm Dottie. Get it? Dottie?" She waggled her dotted suit at us. "But my real name is Dottie." She let out a huge laugh and pushed us, one hand on each shoulder, into seats in front of a mirror. "Now, don't be afraid of a little makeup," she said, taking out a sponge and smearing white down my forehead and across my cheek. "It washes right off. Yes, it does." *Swipe. Swipe-swipe.* She was fast at putting on makeup. So fast that my face was finished before my brain had even caught up that she'd started. She turned and began smearing Chip's face. "Do you want to be a happy clown or a sad one? You know, never mind, you look like a clown with a teeny-tiny mouth. Here, let me get some white on those lips."

Some more smearing and swiping, and a whole lot of foghorny talking, and Dottie stepped back, revealing Chip and I to ourselves in the mirror. He was a puckering clown. I was an angry one with lines between my eyebrows. She surveyed us, beaming.

"Well, if you two don't look just about perfect. Let me find you some clothes. It's bull night tonight. Rodeo clowns must know how to distract a bull, of course. But don't worry, we won't make you go out there by yourselves on your first night. We'll have JoJo go with you. Here." She tossed two outfits at us and brushed off her hands. Neither Chip nor I had spoken a word since she took hold of us. "You two change, and I'm going to round up JoJo for ya."

She left. Chip and I both sat on our benches, stunned.

"What just happened?" I asked.

"I think we enrolled in clown school," Chip said. Then to himself, "Oddly, not the first time for me."

Harvey appeared in a black-and-white-checkered three-piece suit, red wig in place. One pocket of his jacket was stuffed with deflated balloons. He actually looked pretty good.

"You're a clown?" I asked. "Why were you acting so shifty about it? I mean, why the hoodie and looking over your shoulder and carrying your wig in a bag and everything?"

He concentrated on the toes of his huge black

shoes, shuffling them in the dirt and kicking little clouds of dust into the air. "Because it's embarrassing enough to be the balloon-animal guy," he said. "I didn't want Buckley or Colton finding out that I was a clown, too. They already tease me as it is."

Helen Heirmauser wouldn't have allowed that, I caught myself thinking, and then thought, *How on earth would you know, Thomas? You never met the woman!*

"But I'm really, really good at clowning," Harvey said. "It's my gift. And I like it. And I want to keep doing it. Maybe forever. I'm just not ready for everyone to know about it." He glanced up. "Are you going to tell?"

I shook my head. "I'm a magician, so I think I totally get it," I said. I pointed to Chip with my thumb. "And he sings into pizza, so you're safe there."

Harvey let out a relieved breath. "Thanks."

Dottie came back, roaring something about the ring being ready to go and Billy the Bull looking especially ornery tonight. I felt cold all the way to my toes.

"You two ready to feel the spotlight?" she asked.

"Not really," I said, at the same time that Chip furiously nodded and cried, "Absolutely!"

She laughed. "You'll love it. Come on."

Dottie pulled us out of our chairs and led us into what I guessed was a bull-riding ring. There were hoof imprints all over the ground. And a very large stain, which, no matter what it was, I planned to avoid at all costs.

"The clown's job is to distract the bull so it doesn't hurt the rider," Dottie explained. "And to be funny in the process. Watch me." She raced around the ring, making exaggerated scared faces and holding on to her wig, dodging an imaginary bull. Finally, she jumped over the ring wall and popped up just on the outside. "See? Now you try."

I would like to say that Chip and I reluctantly moped around the ring, or possibly that we ran and kept running until we made our escape through a back door, but the truth was it was kind of fun spinning through the ring, making faces, whooping and hollering, doing somersaults, and stopping to shake our hips.

"Very good," Dottie yelled when we were finished. She squawked a horn a few times for applause. "Not bad at all for first-timers. Come on out here and watch what it's like with a real bull. Here comes JoJo now."

A skinny clown in raggedy clothes came sauntering into the ring from the other side. He took off his top hat, which had holes in it, and bowed to the audience. We cheered. Soon there was a clanking noise and a moo, and the next thing we knew, a real, live, actual bull was galloping into the ring.

JoJo sprang into action, taunting the bull until it rushed him, and then scraping away just in the nick of time. After a few misses, the bull had had enough. It lowered its head and charged. JoJo tossed his hat into the air and sprinted for the barrel in the center of the ring. He jumped in just as the bull dipped its head and smashed into it with its horns. The barrel rolled. The bull smashed into it again, and with a hollow *clop* it rolled again, coming closer to us. The bull kept after it, rolling and rolling the barrel until I started to get afraid that it would roll right through the wall. But then the bull seemed to get bored and lumbered away, sniffing the ground for something to eat.

We applauded JoJo, who popped up out of the barrel, took a deep bow, and ran over to us.

I squinted, turning my head to one side. "Chip," I said, elbowing his side, "is there something about JoJo that looks familiar to you?"

Chip squinted and turned his head to one side, too. "Yeah," he said. "But I can't quite put my finger on it. Is it the way he walks?"

"No, it's more like the way he stands still." And then JoJo made right for us, and within just a few steps, I saw it. The gray curly hair tufting out from under his wig. The slender legs with the toes that pointed just slightly in. The victorious smile I knew so well.

"That's not JoJo," I cried, pointing. "That's my grandma Jo!"

TRICK #30

THERE'S A COIN IN YOUR EAR

Grandma Jo made me promise not to tell Mom that she was a rodeo clown. I made her promise not to tell Mom that Chip and I had biked all the way across town.

"Yeah, what's the deal with that?" Grandma Jo asked. "Since when are you interested in clowning? If you ask me, you're a little too serious for it. You're more like your grandpa. A natural magician. Magicians can be serious, and it only makes their show more interesting. Serious clowns, though, are kind of a drag."

We were strolling through Walmart, lazily pushing a cart while we looked at irons and shower curtains and big plastic tubs and all kinds of things we didn't need. Mom was grocery shopping, but she made me promise not to let Grandma Jo out of my sight.

"I don't want to be a clown," I said. "Not that there's anything wrong with clowning. It was kind of fun. And you're really good at it."

Grandma Jo looked pleased with herself. "Yeah, I suppose I am, aren't I?" She picked up a saucepan, examined it, and put it back on the shelf. "So, what were you doing there if you weren't interested in clowning?"

"You promise not to tell Mom or Dad?"

"We've already been through this. I promised. I'll keep my word."

"Chip and I thought that Harvey Hinkle was the one who stole the statue from my school. We were trying to steal it back."

"Harvey Hinkle, huh? And you rode your bicycle all the way across town and put on a clown costume to prove it." Grandma Jo stopped and leaned over the cart handle so she could study me. "You really didn't do it, did you?" she asked. "You didn't steal the statue." A declaration, not a question.

I shook my head, and out of nowhere, tears sprang into my eyes. I blinked rapidly to make them go away. "I've been trying to tell everyone that."

Grandma Jo chewed the side of her lip. "Well, then, you should prove it."

"I've been trying to," I said. We began walking again,

and I was thankful for it, because looking Grandma Jo in the face was making me want to cry. The last place a dude wants to get caught crying is at the store with his grandma. "But every lead I follow is a bad one. I don't know what to do next."

Grandma Jo picked up a purple Styrofoam jack-o-lantern and tossed it into the cart. It still seemed a little early for Halloween stuff, but Grandma Jo liked to be ahead of the game. She also liked to buy strange stuff just to hear Mom squawk. She liked to do a lot of things just to make Mom squawk. Sometimes I thought maybe a Making Mom Squawk Adventure was what Grandma Jo did when she wasn't busy with any real adventures. "Seems to me you've just been looking in the wrong places," she said.

"But I don't know where else to look. Even Chip has been wrong, and I don't think that happens very often." I tossed a bag of candy corn into the cart, because Grandma Jo could get away with it, and later, when I smuggled the bag into my room, she wouldn't get all yelly at me about sugar and my teeth and yak-yak-yak. "Where should I look?"

She stopped again and bent to gaze right into my eyes. A toddler was screaming in the cart next to us. "At the other hand," she said.

"I don't get it."

"You're a magician, Thomas. You know all about the

264

other hand. Here, make this disappear." She handed me a small candle.

I looked around nervously. "I don't think it's a good idea to make things disappear in a store," I said.

"Just do it." She closed my palm around the candle. "I'll bail you out."

I sighed and positioned the candle in the palm of my hand. I reached over with my other hand, and with a flourish of my fingers, grabbed air to make it look like I was grabbing the candle, but kept the candle in the original hand. When I dramatically showed Grandma Jo my empty "grabbing" hand, I shoved the candle in my front pocket with the other. "Gone," I said, spreading my fingers and showing her my palms.

She reached over and tapped my pocket. "I was married to a magician for forty years. I know it's all about making people look . . . at the other . . . hand." She opened her hand dramatically just as I had done. I still had no idea what she meant. Maybe she'd chased one too many bulls or landed on her head in the skate park or something.

I pulled the candle out of my pocket and put it back on the shelf. We started moving again.

"So you think I'm a pretty good rodeo clown, huh?" Grandma Jo asked as we turned down the lightbulb aisle.

"Really good," I said. "That bull didn't stand a chance."

"I suppose you're right," she said. "But I'm thinking of taking up rock climbing instead. Do not tell your mother."

I wouldn't dream of it.

7

My parents always made me go to the basement when I wanted to try out a new trick using Grandpa Rudy's chemicals. They figured there were tons of ways for chemistry magic to go wrong, especially when you're using recordings from two decades ago, and if I was going to mess up, at least I would only mess up the concrete floor and some old boxes full of Christmas ornaments. And there was a rule: if I messed up in a smelly way, I had to leave my clothes in the basement and hope that I wouldn't run into Grandma Jo or Erma or one of Erma's girly friends while I ran to my bedroom for new clothes. I was determined to never have a smelly mistake.

I needed some time alone to sort through everything. Grandma Jo was right. I was looking for the head in the wrong places. But I still didn't understand what she meant by looking at the other hand and how that would lead me to the bust.

In the meantime, I had something called phenolphthalein to mess with.

I smoothed out Grandpa Rudy's notes and set them on the floor next to my trunk. I pulled out the three plastic cups he'd left in there, along with some little vials marked NaOH and HCl and one marked $(C_3H_3NaO_2)n$. One of these days I would learn how to say the names of these chemicals out loud; they made me feel like a mad scientist with all kinds of power in my hands.

According to Grandpa Rudy, if I mixed these things just right, I could turn water pink, then back to clear, and then make it disappear altogether. The big wow moment.

So far I had yet to get it right.

But I was in no hurry to do anything else, so I tried over and over again, the words "Look at the other hand" swirling around in the plastic cups with the liquid. What did she mean?

I poured the phenolphthalein into some water and started over. And that was when it hit me.

Quickly, I dug through the trunk until I found Grandpa Rudy's lucky fifty-cent piece—the one he used to wow Erma and me with by pulling it out of our ears. I palmed it, using my thumb to hold it in place. Using my other hand, I grabbed air over my palm, manipulating my fingers so that it looked like I grabbed the coin. Meanwhile, my other hand, still holding the coin, casually dangled at my side.

When Grandpa Rudy would do this trick for Erma and me, we would be so busy looking at the grabbing hand— sometimes even yanking on it and turning it over to see where the fifty-cent piece had gone—we totally didn't even see what the other hand was doing. And that was the hand that was tricking us. We were seeing the magic, not the trick. But at the same time, it was so obvious. Everyone who ever saw a sleight-of-hand trick knew that the "disappeared" object was simply hidden . . . by the hand nobody was looking at.

I did the trick again.

Look at the other hand.

And again.

Look at the other hand.

I repeated the trick over and over, Grandma Jo's voice morphing into Grandpa Rudy's. *"The thing about magic is, people will see what they want to see,"* he always said. *"So you have to make them want to see magic."*

I dropped the fifty-cent piece and let it roll, staring at a Grandpa Rudy who wasn't really there. "Make them look away from the trick," I said aloud.

Then, forgetting all about the pink and clear and disappearing chemicals, I raced upstairs to find Erma.

I knew who stole Helen Heirmauser's head.

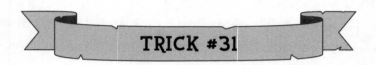

TRICK #31

A HAT FULL OF EVIDENCE

"Are you sure?" Erma kept asking. She was sitting cross-legged on her overly ruffled and overly pink and overly everything bed, picking at the whiskers of her favorite stuffed kitty, which she'd named Kitty. She also had a walrus named Wallyrus and a parrot named Bird. Erma was not all that creative.

"I'm positive," I kept saying, trying not to touch anything, for fear that I would be covered with sparkles for the rest of my life.

"Tell me again."

I paced across her pink throw rug, back and forth, laying out points by tapping my finger in my palm. "He knew the exact weight and measurements of the statue. He knew about the darker spot on the pedestal, even though I didn't tell him, and he led me to the exact spot where the pedestal was, and he doesn't even go to that school. He was the one who wanted to break in and confront Byron. He was the one who was eating cheese curls in the back of the vending-machine van. He was the one who wasted two whole nights by taking us to rodeo clown school." I stopped pacing and faced her. "Erma, don't you see? Chip Mason is the other hand. He was making me look away from the trick."

"So what are you going to do?" she asked.

"You mean, what are *we* going to do?"

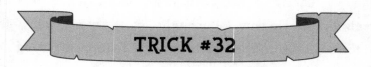

TRICK #32

ABRACONFESSION!

Chip Mason was not an easy guy to spy on. Mostly because Chip Mason was always around. Every time Erma and I tried to get close to his house, he would bound out the front door, practicing cartwheels or reciting poetry or flopping face-first into the grass to get a bug's-eye view of grasshopper-land. We ended up having to act like we were coming over to see what he was doing, even though all we could think about was how he was letting me be blamed for something he did.

But we needed proof, so we kept trying.

"How about I distract him while you look in his window?" Erma asked one day. "Maybe the statue is just sitting out somewhere."

"How are you going to do that?"

"I don't know. I could pretend I have a crush."

We both watched as Chip Mason had a conversation about former president Taft with a Popsicle.

"I'm not sure he knows what a crush is," I said.

"No, probably not."

"You could fall off your bike and get hurt," I proposed.

Erma slugged me in the side. "That's a terrible suggestion. I'm not getting hurt for your stupid head statue."

"You shouldn't let anybody hear you say that," I said. "Or everyone's going to think you stole it."

"Not for long," Erma said, and before I could argue, she skipped over to Chip. "Can I have a bite, Chippy Wippy?"

Chippy Wippy? I fought the urge to barf. Chip refused, looking as confused and grossed out as I was feeling. I almost felt sorry for him, but . . . well. He was a thief and a terrible friend. And a liar. He deserved to be Ermafied.

Louis XIV: Eradication by Ermafication. Crushed by an Erma crush.

She giggled, loud and long. "You're so cute, Chippy Wippy. Tell me that story about the pizza opera again."

Okay, maybe I had to give Erma some credit. Because that was a really long, really boring story. Nobody in their right mind wanted to hear it. And Chippy Wippy loved to tell it.

He bit off a hunk of his Popsicle and chewed—another sign that I shouldn't have trusted him; who bites a Popsicle?— and then started talking. Erma leaned into his shoulder, as if she were captivated by his every word, providing me with cover. I slithered through the hedges and across the street, through Chip's weeping willow tree, and to the first window I found.

A laundry room. A really messy laundry room. Clothes and hangers and bottles of detergent everywhere, piles of blankets, and panty hose hanging from the top of the door. But no statue.

I stole around the side of the house, most of the windows way too high for me to see through. I let myself through a gate and into the backyard. Old Huck Mason used to have a dog. A scruffy white one that barked a lot and licked your fingers through the fence if you let him. But that dog was gone for a long time now, and all that was in the backyard were a couple of trees and a wooden porch. There were three windows visible from the porch. I climbed the steps as quietly as I could and peered through the first one. Just curtains I couldn't see through. The second one looked at the back of a cabinet. I cupped my hands and looked through the third. Then jumped and ducked.

It was a kitchen, and Chip Mason's mom was sitting at the table, her head in her hand, her other hand holding a coffee mug. She didn't see me. Slowly, I stood again, just enough to peek through the window. She wasn't holding her head in her hand after all. She was sleeping with her cheek propped on her hand, her other hand loosely wrapped around the cup.

As if she could sense that someone was watching her, she

jerked awake, knocking her cup over. She jumped up, swiping at the brown stain that had soaked into her pant leg. She looked confused and irritated. And really, really tired.

She went over to the counter for a towel, and I took the opportunity to study the room. No Heirmauser head.

I crept back down the porch steps, thinking maybe I should just give up. But there was one more window on the other side of the house.

It was just above the air-conditioning unit.

I climbed on top of the unit, rose up on my toes, and peered in. It was a dining room. Only it wasn't exactly a dining room. It was a dining room that had been turned into a bedroom. There was a bed—the kind you see in hospitals—on the far wall, a shriveled-looking old man lying in it. I jumped and ducked back under the windowsill, almost falling off the air conditioner, but then I realized that the old man had been sleeping, his mouth open in a wide "O." Slowly, I rose back up on my tiptoes.

There was a tube going into the old man's nose. He was very pale. His skin looked loose and like it was just kind of draped over his bones. He wore a thin T-shirt and was covered with a tan blanket. Next to his bed was a table. On it was a glass with a straw and several pill bottles.

Old Huck Mason. Grandma Jo had said he'd invented mean. But in that bed, he didn't look so mean at all. He just looked sick.

And I kind of felt sick for spying on him like that. It didn't feel right. Even if Chip deserved to be spied on, Old Huck Mason hadn't done anything wrong, and he deserved his privacy. I started to lower myself and just give up, but a glint of sunlight bounced off something on a table on the other side of Old Huck's bed.

A forehead.

Beneath unruly, wavy hair.

Wide, raving eyes.

A mouth held open in a perpetual scream.

All frozen in bronze, and somehow managing to look worse than the sick guy lying next to it.

I was right: Chip Mason was the Helen Heirmauser Head of Horror bandit.

Erma looked like she was half asleep by the time I got back to our driveway, and Chip was still two scenes away from the end of Act I.

I slunk around Dad's car and caught her attention, giving her a thumbs-up, followed by a slash across the throat using my forefinger, and then motioned for her to come home. We needed to come up with a plan on how we would approach Chip and get the statue back, safe and sound. We would sit down tonight and think of something intricate and precise. No room for error. Maybe we would even have graphs.

Her eyes narrowed, and she stood up like a shot.

"I think we're done here," I heard her say.

Chip's Popsicle, forgotten, was dripping down his hand. "Okay," he said uncertainly. "It picks up in the second act, though."

She stomped one foot one time, true Erma-style, and I knew then that this was going to be bad.

"You're a thief!" she cried, pointing at him like they did in old detective movies.

So much for coming up with a plan. And just when I'd started to get excited about the graph part.

I started across the street, my heart in my throat. Now that I knew where the head was, I was suddenly really nervous about getting it back. What if he denied taking it? What if he argued and refused to hand it over? What if he was wearing deadly ninja socks and went all foot tornado on us?

Louis XIV: Finished by a foot tornado to the chops.

"Huh?" The Popsicle fell off the stick and landed on his leg. He brushed it into the grass.

"We know you stole that statue. You're a liar and a thief, and a really, really bad friend!" She jabbed her finger at him with every word. "And we're going to tell on you!"

Ah. I hadn't considered that. We could just . . . tell. Sometimes fifth graders could be pretty smart in ways we wouldn't think of.

Chip saw me coming up into his yard and licked his lips nervously. He stood. A drip of orange Popsicle trailed down his leg. His eyes darted between me and Erma. "I don't know what you're talking about," he said.

"You do, too, and we're going to call the FBI on you, right, Thomas?"

"Well, I don't know about the FBI . . ."

"Then we'll call the president!" *Jab-jab-jab.*

"The president probably wouldn't really care," I said.

"Then we'll call the school."

I thought about it. "They would probably care."

She started hopping up and down on her toes, the way she always did when she got, as my mom called it, "overly excited." Clearly, Erma was having an Overly Excited Adventure, and I knew from experience that if I didn't calm her down soon, there would be no saving Chip from her.

"We'll call the school, and they'll call the police," she said. "And they'll call the FBI. And they'll come out with helicopters and sirens and big dogs with huge teeth." She bared her teeth at him and growled. "And they'll tell those dogs to—"

"Okay, okay, I took it!" Chip's face had gotten very red, and his eyes were swimmy-looking. Erma's mouth clapped shut, and she stopped hopping. She probably hadn't expected him to cave in so quickly. "I took it for my grandpa. I'm guilty, and you should just . . . take me to jail." His chin quivered. "I'll go get my jail socks."

Erma threw her head back. "Aha! I knew it!" She started dancing around and singing, "We solved the cri-ime. We solved the cri-ime."

To be fair, *I* solved the crime—she only got me locked in a cheese-curl truck and distracted Chip for a few minutes. But it didn't seem like a good time to point that out, because when I looked at Chip again, two big tears were hanging off his chin. "We solved the cri-ime. We solved the—"

"That's enough, Erma," I said.

She stopped dancing and glared at me. "So what are we going to do? Turn him in? Call the news? Pound him into the ground like a nail?"

I waved my hand at her, the way Dad does when he wants her to stop talking. "Go home, Erma. Thanks for the help, but I've got it from here."

"You're going to turn him in, right, Thomas? You're at least going to tell Mom."

I glanced at her. "Just go home. I'll let you know when I get there."

Erma's shoulders drooped in a sulk, but she trudged through the grass and back across the street. Once home, she plopped onto our porch step and rested her chin in her hands, watching us closely.

I turned back to Chip. More tears had gathered on his chin. There were so many things I wanted to say. I had imagined myself yelling at the thief when I finally found him. Dancing like Erma did. Maybe even calling him a few names that would make Mom want to take me on a Wash Out Your Filthy Mouth with Soap Adventure. But Chip looked so pathetic and sorry, all I could say was . . .

"Why?"

He shrugged, his throat working, his face crumpling until it looked like a red, splotchy paper ball. He looked like he wanted to talk but couldn't get the words out.

"Why, Chip? Why did you take it?"

He only shrugged again, more tears falling down his cheeks. I felt a surge of anger and dismay that made my insides feel like concrete.

"Say something!" I ran my hands through my hair, and then pounded my fist into my palm. "How could you do that to me? All this time, knowing what was happening to me at school, knowing that my own parents—my own parents, Chip!—thought I was the thief. I got suspended! You helped me break into the school to accuse an innocent man. You made me go to rodeo clown school. And all this time, the statue was sitting in your dining room! Why?"

"Because he was getting really bad," Chip finally answered. He choked out a sob. I stopped pacing. "My grandpa Huck. He's not going to get better. Ever. And he was in a lot of pain. And he was sad and mad all the time, and my mom was sad and mad all the time, and I just . . . I thought the statue of his aunt Helen might cheer him up."

Aunt . . . Helen?

"Wait. Did you say 'Aunt Helen'?"

Chip nodded. "Grandpa Huck was her favorite nephew. And also her favorite student. Mom says when she died is when he got cranky all the time. He really misses her."

"His *aunt* Helen," I repeated, because in all this time it never occurred to me that the Great Helen Heirmauser was ever anything more than a legend and a statue. She was a real person with a real family who loved her and missed her.

"I only planned to borrow it, until . . . well, you know."

"Until he dies," I said. I flashed onto the image of the old, sick man that I'd seen through Chip's window. He looked really, really sick—so sick that it had kind of scared me. I couldn't help wondering what it must have been like to be Chip, living with him being so sick right in the same house. It was probably really scary and really sad all the time. But you never would have known that by the way Chip acted. Chip was . . . kind of strong.

Chip nodded, squeezing out more tears. "I didn't think it would be such a big deal. I was going to give it back. I told my mom that the school loaned it to me, and she's so busy with Grandpa Huck, she hasn't heard anything about it being stolen. I figured by the time she knew anything, I would have it back on its pedestal, and everything would be fine. It would be an interesting note in my baby book."

"But it wasn't fine," I said. "It wasn't fine, because I got blamed for it. And you let me take the heat. You even pretended you were helping me solve the crime, when the whole time you were the criminal."

"I felt really bad about that," Chip said. "And I almost gave myself up. But the thing is . . ."

"What?" I prodded. "The thing is what?"

"Well, you were being my friend," he burst out, turning his palms up helplessly. "And I never really had one of those before. I'm so . . . different. Nobody likes me because I don't think or talk or act or dress like everyone else. Nobody even talks to me at Boone Public. I was having so much fun with you, trying to solve the crime, I almost forgot that I was the person we were trying to catch. I didn't want it to end. I wanted to keep having a friend. For the first time ever."

"Oh," I said, because what else could you say to something like that?

"But now you hate me, and I don't blame you," Chip said, and he sat back down in the grass, almost landing right in the Popsicle puddle. He looked small and pathetic down there.

"I don't hate you," I said. "I'm pretty mad at you right now, but I don't hate you."

"But you're going to turn me in," he said. "And I'm going to get into huge trouble."

Something about that made me feel kind of squicky in ways I couldn't quite describe. But that wasn't my fault, was it? I didn't make Chip Mason take the statue. I didn't steal and then let someone else take the blame. I was innocent in all of this, and I had already gotten into huge trouble. *Chip's* huge trouble. And he'd let me.

"You should have thought about that before you took the statue," I said, and walked toward Erma, who was now standing on the front porch with her arms crossed.

Grandma Jo was sitting on the couch, watching a game show with a bowl of cheese puffs in her lap. I stormed over to her. Erma trailed behind me.

"You knew," I said.

Grandma Jo pointed at the TV. "Oh, you're just in time to see this guy win the grand prize. It's a zip-lining trip."

"You knew," I repeated.

She dug into the bowl and pulled out a handful of cheese puffs. "I think I'll talk to Barf about taking a zip-lining trip. Wouldn't it be fun to skim across the tops of the trees?" She glided her free hand through the air, then held the other palm open toward me. "Cheese puff?"

Erma grabbed one, and I glared at her.

"You knew it was Chip Mason."

Grandma Jo chewed thoughtfully, and then nodded. "Yep, I did."

"Why didn't you say anything?"

"You were handling it." She picked up the remote and adjusted the volume, louder. "Oh, it's back. Watch, he's about to win."

I took the remote from her and muted the sound. "I was in so much trouble. I got suspended. I got grounded. I lost friends. I almost got killed by a bull."

She shrugged. "I didn't say you were handling it *well*. And don't be such a ninny. That bull was never going to kill you. Maybe just break a few bones or something." She leaned forward and set the cheese-puff bowl on the coffee table. Erma immediately went for it. "Look, Thomas. I would have come to your rescue if it had gotten bad enough."

"Bad enough?" I raged. "It wasn't already bad enough?"

She shook her head. "You were fine. Better than fine, actually. You were having adventures. You were going places and thinking about things and taking risks, and there was pink in your cheeks." She pinched her own cheeks to display. "I hadn't seen that since you left your old school. I had been starting to worry about you in that stuffy bow tie and vest, looking like a miserable little old man."

I started to argue with her, but she was sort of right. Trying to solve the mystery had felt a little bit like an adventure, and there was a part of me that wondered if I would be bored now that the statue, and the thief, had been found.

Grandma Jo reached forward and plucked the remote out of my hand. "You were having fun, Thomas. That's a good thing. You should do it more often." She pressed the mute button, but the show was over. "Oh, rats. I missed it. Did you see, Ermie? Did he win?"

Erma shrugged, shoveling more cheese puffs into her mouth. "You gonna tell Mom, Thomas?" she asked around a mouthful. "Thomas?"

I heard her, but I kind of didn't hear her, because my brain was too busy talking to me, telling me that Grandma Jo was right, whether I liked it or not. I thought about Chip's mom, asleep at the kitchen table, and his grandpa in that bed. And Chip playing I spy with me while eating ice cream like nothing at all was wrong. Having fun. For the first time in a long time for me. For the first time maybe ever for him.

I felt kind of sorry for him. My friend.

Wow. I had begun to think of Chip Mason as my friend.

"Thomas? Are you telling?" Erma asked again.

But I didn't answer her. I just turned around and went right back outside.

17

Chip was still sitting in the grass, where I'd left him. He'd broken his Popsicle stick into several pieces and was using blades of grass to tie them together in the shape of a person. He looked up as I approached.

I marched right up to him. "I was having fun with you, too."

He blinked up at me. I tried to ignore how much his nose was running onto his upper lip, because if I looked too long at something like that, my stomach got all jumpy.

"Really?"

I nodded. "Yeah."

"Are you still going to turn me in?"

If I turned Chip in, he would be in huge trouble. And the whole town would turn on him—I knew this because of what had happened to me.

And, because he was my friend, I didn't want it to happen to Chip. He was only trying to make his grandpa feel better, after all.

"Maybe not," I said. "I might have an idea."

TRICK #33

GONE

Erma couldn't believe I wouldn't let her tell anyone what Chip had done.

"I can't belieeeve it, Thomas," she said. "I just can't belieeeve it."

"Well, believe it, Erma, because I'm not turning him in."

We were in my bedroom, where I was gathering some materials together to perform the greatest trick I'd ever performed. Grandpa Rudy had been on the verge of perfecting it right before he died. After he'd gone, I had promised myself that I would finish the job. And I'd gotten pretty good at it. Even if the silver pennies hadn't convinced Mom that I was a magic genius, this trick would have. It wasn't everyone who could make an invisibility cloak.

Now I had a real reason for using it. And I had the

supplies—four simple lenses of different focal lengths. I'd never tried it on such a grand scale, but it seemed easy enough. The hard part would be getting the head there in the first place. And getting Erma not to spill the beans.

"Well, there's no reason I can't still turn him in," she said.

I sighed and continued packing my bag. "Okay, what do you want?"

"What do you mean?"

"What can I give you to make you not tell?" I asked.

She thought about it. "You have to play with me sometime," she said.

"That's it? Fine. I'll play with you."

"And it has to be what I want to play."

"Okay, whatever."

"And you have to let Arthura play with us."

I gritted my teeth. I hoped Chip appreciated what I was doing for him. "Okay," I said. "Deal. Now will you keep your trap shut?"

She mimed zipping her lips together and then locking them with a key.

I finished packing my bag, then went to bed, hoping Chip and I could pull this off in the morning.

Chip had the idea to put the head in a wagon and to cover it with the rolled-up newspapers his Grandpa Huck had kept in his recycling. I worked on my tie-wad while he worked on that.

I threw on my vest and gobbled down my cereal before Mom and Dad even came to the breakfast table. Erma was to tell them I'd gone with Chip on his newspaper delivery route "to learn responsibility and see the error of my ways so that school would let me back in and I could continue my education without incident." Chip helped us write that. He was wearing his speech-writing socks at the time, and I thought it came out pretty good. Maybe there was something to this sock business.

By the time they knew it was a lie, Chip and I would have already made the head reappear, and I would be back in school, and they would be so happy that they would forget all about the lie in the first place. Or at least that was the plan.

I biked ahead of Chip so I could set up the lenses before anyone got there. That meant I had to hang on to the vines outside the bathroom window we'd broken into before and climb up the side of the building, then squeeze myself through the tiny hole that Chip had gone through. Just like Chip's, my foot landed in the toilet. But I was in too much of a hurry to care. And it was mostly flushed, anyway.

The school was dark and empty. I thought maybe I could hear a faint growling sound coming from the basement—NAAAW!—but it was probably just in my head. I hoisted my backpack tighter and squish-ran through the hallways, all the way to the vestibule.

The pedestal was, of course, empty. I set up my lenses, hoping to hide them where nobody could see them.

I had just finished and was standing back admiring my work—maybe I really was gifted at this magic stuff—when I heard howling. Very loud howling.

I squish-raced back through the hallways to the bathroom and opened the window. Chip was standing on the ground, still clutching the handle of the wagon, his head thrown back and his eyes closed. He took a deep breath, then let out another howl. "Ow-ow-owoooooo!"

"You were supposed to make an owl noise," I hissed.

He opened his eyes. A smile spread across his face. "Oh, hey, Thomas." He waved. "I'm here."

"You were supposed to make an owl noise," I repeated.

"Huh?"

"An owl. You were supposed to be an owl."

"Oh." He scratched his chin a little. "I thought you said I was supposed to howl."

I grunted. "Never mind, just pass it up."

Carefully, Chip dug the newspapers out of the wagon and uncovered the statue. He cradled it in his arms, rolled the wagon directly under the window, stepped up into the wagon, and held the statue over his head. He could barely lift it, and I had to lean way out to get my hands on it. For a second, the statue wobbled, slipping from our fingers. I gripped it harder and pulled it inside.

This was the first time I'd ever touched the statue. It was really the first time I'd even looked at it up close. It had been the thing that had taken my life apart, and would be the thing to put it back together. It was the most important thing in my world at that moment. It was a memorial to an amazing woman who was important to a lot of people.

And it was still the ugliest thing I'd ever laid eyes on.

I shivered and poked my head through the window. "Okay, I'll be right back. Don't move."

"Aye-aye, captain," Chip said, saluting me.

My breathing was fast and loud, and I was pretty sure

my heart was galloping ahead of me down the hall, but I forced myself to squish-walk back to the entryway so I didn't accidentally drop the bust and break it. Carefully, carefully, I placed it back on the pedestal and positioned it just so. Then I stepped back and arranged the lenses a touch here, a scooch there, until . . .

"Gone," I whispered as the statue disappeared.

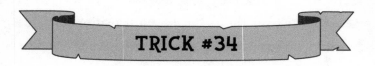

TRICK #34

AND NOW MY ASSISTANT WILL GET CAUGHT

The morning started out as usual. Chip and I watched the school from behind a tree. Miss Munch was the first one into the building, unlocking the front doors with a giant set of keys and then yanking them open. I saw lights flicker on, one by one, and soon Mr. Faboo and Coach Abel and Miss Pancake and Principal Rooster began arriving. They were all just as mopey as ever.

Just wait, I thought. *Just you wait. Your day is about to get a whole lot better.*

Soon cars began to pull up, and students trickled out of them, rushing up the stairs in ones and twos and threes. Next came the buses, loud and hissing, and then the front steps really got busy. My palms sweated uncontrollably as I replayed the plan in my head over and over.

"Now, you think?" Chip asked as the last few students began to pour out of their cars and rush up the steps.

"Wait for the warning bell," I said.

No sooner was it out of my mouth then the familiar tinkle rang through the air. My throat instantly turned into a desert. "Now," I croaked.

Chip and I confidently walked across the lawn and up the steps. We paused only long enough to give each other a you-got-this glance and then, together, pulled open the big front doors. Principal Rooster was right on the other side. He turned, and the welcoming grin he'd been wearing fell from his face.

"Mr. Fallgrout?" he said questioningly. "I thought we agreed that you were on a break for a while."

"Hear me out, Principal Rooster," I said. Chip slipped past me and slithered over to where the closest lens was positioned. "I want to come back to Pennybaker School." Yeah, I couldn't believe I said it, either. And, more so, I couldn't believe I actually meant it. "I think your punishment is unfair." I said it loudly—loud enough to make the vestibule go quiet. Kids stopped on the stairs and watched. Some of them whispered.

Principal Rooster's forehead got very red. "Come to my office and we can discuss this further," he said.

"No, sir," I said loudly. Some kids gasped.

"Mr. Fallgrout, you're making a scene."

"I don't care. I want to know why you suspended me. And it's not about the spitwad war." This time a few kids—especially Wesley—turned their faces and cleared their throats, looking very guilty.

Principal Rooster puckered his lips. His cheeks shook. Finally, he said, "You're right. It's not about that. You were suspended because you stole an important piece of history from this school."

"I did not take that ridiculous head," I said.

"Well, can you explain why it's missing, then?" He gestured to the empty pedestal.

"But it's not missing. See?" Chip's cue. I watched out of the corner of my eye as he nudged one of the lenses just enough to break the illusion.

A long and loud scream pealed through the vestibule. I turned just in time to see Crumbs faint into the arms of the Mop, who fainted into Byron the Basement-Dwelling Country Singer's arms. All heads were turned, all eyes bugged out, as Helen Heirmauser's statue sat, frozen in midscream, for all to see.

Principal Rooster's cheeks puffed and deflated several times. "How did you . . . ? What happened? This was missing just moments ago . . ." He turned to Miss Munch. "It was missing, wasn't it?"

Miss Munch was fumbling with a tissue. "I—I think so, sir," she said.

"Was it not missing?" Principal Rooster said to the crowd at large, which mumbled that, yes, it had been missing, and how on earth could it have just appeared suddenly out of nowhere?

Everyone started talking over one another. Some of the girls were crying. Some boys were standing with their hands over their hearts. A few kids were taking pictures with their phones.

"It's a miracle!" Principal Rooster declared, throwing his hands into the air. "We all just witnessed a miracle."

And then Buckley's voice cut through the crowd. "What is this?" Everyone turned to look at him. He was holding up the lens that Chip had nudged out of place. "And who are you?" he asked Chip. Chip opened and closed his mouth just like a fish that had been caught and pulled out of a lake. He looked at me, panicked.

I cleared my throat and used my best magician's voice, the one that made me think of Grandpa Rudy's shows. "This," I intoned, "is Chip the Great! He is my assistant. And you have all just witnessed the greatest illusion in Pennybaker School history. Alacadabra and ta-da!" I clicked my heels together and swept my arms out, proudly framing the statue.

"You mean . . . this was a magic trick the whole time?" Wesley asked.

"The head was always here?" Miss Munch added.

"You made something disappear for weeks?" Principal Rooster asked, bug-eyed.

I shrugged. "I'm gifted."

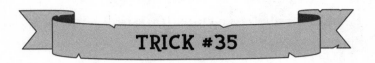

THE HOAX OF THE CENTURY

For a while, there was talk of making a statue out of my head to go next to Helen Heirmauser's, just like Chip had predicted. But, thankfully, I got out of that one when I pointed out that I was not dead yet. And also that my hair wasn't quite as frizzy and my mouth didn't open nearly as wide.

Principal Rooster let me back into school immediately, my suspension lifted. He escorted me to first period, asking me question after question about how I'd pulled off such an elaborate trick. I mostly mumbled stuff that sounded technical and fudged my way through the rest of it, but he ate it up.

The newspaper came to my house. They took photos of me with Mom and Dad and Erma. But not Grandma Jo, because while everyone was so busy fussing over me, she had taken the opportunity to go on a whitewater rafting trip with some new friends she called Toaster, Echo, and Jungle Pete. The newspaper article headline read, "Boone County Genius Pulls Off Hoax of the Century." I had to stand next to the head for another picture. It was still horrifying, but it had kind of started to grow on me.

The day that I revealed my "big hoax" to the school, Wesley, Buckley, Colton, Flea, and Owen called me to their lunch table. I went over warily.

"Top o' the mornin', my good laddie," Wesley said. He'd broken out his Irish brogue, which could only mean one thing: things were right again between us.

"Hey," I said.

"Have a seat, have a seat." Wesley stood and brushed off the bench next to him.

"Have some pudding." Flea offered me a bowl of chocolate. I gazed into it to see if he'd drowned some flies in it or something.

"Don't worry, we didn't do anything to it," Buckley said, leaning into my ear. Not that I would trust anything Buckley had to say.

"Or maybe we did," Colton joked, elbowing Buckley.

"All right, all right. No more acting the maggot," Wesley said.

I pushed the bowl away. "You put maggots in it?"

"No, laddie. 'Acting the maggot' is an Irish way of saying

'playing around.' I'm telling these two dopes to stop playing around. We've got business to attend to."

"We do?"

He nodded and smiled. "I've got something for you." He reached into his back pocket. "I believe this belongs to you, sir."

"My straw!" I said, taking it. Or at least a pretty good reproduction. "Does this mean . . . ?"

Wesley clapped me on the back. "Yes, indeed, boyo. You're back on the team. And the war's still on. We'll even reinstate you as team captain."

"And we're sorry," Flea said, settling onto the bench next to me. "About that whole ambush thing."

Owen's face popped up from behind a laptop across

the table. "Yeah. We acted like real jerks. We should've trusted you."

"Do you forgive us?" Wesley asked in a baby voice.

I smiled and slipped the straw into my pocket. "Of course I do. Oh, and Wesley?"

"Yeah?"

"You can have your brilliant Nationwide History Day topic back. I've got a new one. Mr. Faboo already approved it."

"What is it?" Owen asked. "The history of pudding and other gelatinous desserts?" He stuffed a spoonful of pudding into his mouth.

"Yuck," Flea said, staring into his own pudding. "When you put it that way . . ."

"Nope," I said. "I'm studying Eugene Francois Vidocq."

They all exchanged glances, then looked back at me questioningly.

I grinned, holding a spoonful of pudding. "The first-ever detective."

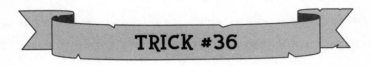

TRICK #36

ENCORE! ENCORE!

I was heading out for target practice at Pettigrew Park when I saw Chip in his front yard. He was wearing a pair of tan slacks and a white shirt, and his hair was slicked back. He was doing some sort of victory dance as he walked toward me.

In a pair of penny loafers.

"Guess what, Thomas?" Chip hollered, way too loudly for someone who was just a few feet away from me. His hands were behind his back.

"You're wearing your dancing socks?"

He pulled up his pant legs to show bare ankles. "Nope."

"You're studying the history of tan clothes?"

"Nuh-unh." He was grinning so wide it looked like it hurt.

"I give up."

"Behold!" he crowed, his arms flying out. In one hand he held a brown vest. In the other, a brown bow tie. "You're looking at the newest sixth grader at Pennybaker School for the Uniquely Gifted. And because I'm your assistant, Chip the Great, we're in all the same classes. Isn't that the best?"

There was a time when I would have thought that was anything but the best. In fact, there was a time, and not that long ago, when I would have thought having to hang around with Chip Mason all day, every day was the absolute worst.

But now it seemed like a pretty cool thing.

"Congratulations, Chip. We should celebrate. Do you have any straws in your house?" I asked. "And something a little more . . . camouflaged?"

He ran inside to get one and came back outside wearing a very hairy olive green suit. He looked like a deranged Muppet.

"I didn't mean actual camouflage," I said.

"Do you know what this is called?" he asked.

"Ugly?"

"It's called a ghillie suit. Or, if you're in the Australian army, you might refer to it as a yowie suit—a yowie, of course, being a Bigfoot-type monster."

I started walking, Chip trailing along next to me, sucking up all the air with facts about the ridiculous outfit he was wearing.

"It's a little-known fact that ghillie suits were invented by Scottish gamekeepers, and that a *gille*, in Gaelic, means 'lad.'" He said "lad" in a heavy accent.

"Say that again."

"Lad."

"Now say it with an 'i-e' at the end."

He twisted up his mouth. "Laddie," he said.

I nodded. "I have this friend I'm going to introduce you to. His name's Wesley."

I told him all about Wesley and Flea and Owen, and even about Patrice Pillow and Mr. Faboo, as we walked to the park. Chip seemed to get more and more excited about Pennybaker School with every detail. It was as if he just knew he was going to fit right in. And somehow, I thought, he probably would.

"I already taught myself how to tie a bow tie," he boasted.

"Really? You might want to teach me."

"Okay!" He bounced around me in circles. "Did you know that the first person to wear the bow tie for fashion was—"

"Louis XIV," I finished for him.

He stopped, his eyes wide. "How did you know that?"

I shrugged. "He used to be my mortal enemy."

CURTAIN CALL TRICK

FLYING OBJECTS

"So, I just blow on the straw?" Chip said, turning a white dot around on his tongue.

"You blow *through* the straw," Wesley said. Southern drawl.

"But first you put the paper inside it," Flea said.

I shook my head. "The paper that you're chewing up right now," I said. Sometimes you had to be really clear with Chip Mason about the simplest things.

"Huh," he said, holding the straw up to one eye and peering through. "It seems there would be more aerodynamic ways of doing this." He lowered his straw. "Would you be willing to pause this operation while I go home to fetch my NASA socks?"

"No!" we all said in unison.

I leaned over him. Our voices were echoey inside the entrance to the tunnel slide, which we were all wedged into. "For the last time, your battle socks should be just fine."

"Captain," a voice hissed. I peeked out the end of the slide. A familiar sheet of black hair was looking up at us. "The enemy is approaching."

"Thanks, Patrice," I said. "How long do you think we have?"

"Let me ask the girls." Patrice Pillow scurried off to the monkey bars, where the girl battalion was stationed.

Some of the boys had balked when we gave the girls the front line. But the truth was, the girls had much better aim than we did, mostly because the boys had a tendency to get distracted by spit, and if we were going to combine forces, I wanted to do it very strategically.

And we definitely needed to combine forces for the army we were about to fight.

"They'll be past the merry-go-round in twenty seconds," Patrice called, running through the Pettigrew Park playground. "Man your battle stations! This is not a drill!"

"All right, fellas," I said, loading my straw. "This is what we've been training for. Remember to protect the girls' blind side." I motioned in the direction of the seesaws.

Wesley raised his straw. "For Chip Mason," he said in his important-guy-giving-a-toast voice.

We all raised our straws. "For Chip Mason," we repeated.

"I'm not certain this is a very hygienic endeavor," Chip said.

I got on my knees and peered over the top of the slide. The enemy was approaching. Line after line of soldiers, holding their straws and wearing their Boone Public Middle

School sweatshirts and chanting their Boone Public fight song. Brandon and Paris and Gavin were front and center. I narrowed my eyes and then started down the slide.

"For Pennybaker School!" I shouted.

"For Pennybaker School!" the guys shouted, and one by one, we slid down the slide with our straws loaded.

School sweatshirts and chanting their Boone Public fight song. Brandon and Paris and Gavin were front and center. I narrowed my eyes and then started down the slide.

"For Pennybaker School!" I shouted.

"For Pennybaker School!" the guys shouted, and one by one, we slid down the slide with our straws loaded.

ACKNOWLEDGMENTS

As an author, I get lots of ideas (some good, some not so good, some outright crazy!). That's my job. I write down those ideas in mostly complete sentences that go together to make a story. That is also my job. But to believe in those ideas and take those mostly complete sentences and shift and shape them into a book . . . well, that's sort of magic. In fact, it's an awesome stage show featuring fog machines and rock music and a lot of star magicians. And I would like to thank some of those magicians here.

To Cori Deyoe, for making my ideas and mostly complete sentences appear on the desks of the people who can do the shifting and the shaping. Also, for clapping the loudest at the end of every trick. Even when I drop my wand and my rabbit hops away.

To Brett Wright, for helping me dump those ideas and

mostly complete sentences and some scarves and Ping-Pong balls and a little bit of fire into a top hat and pull out . . . a story. To Sally Morgridge, for making sure nobody can see the cards up my sleeves, and to Sandy Smith, for making sure the tricks look pretty before the smoke clears away—both of you turn those mostly complete sentences into complete sentences, and I thank you for that. To everyone at Bloomsbury who checked and double-checked that my trunk full of tricks was stocked and organized and ready to go: you are all my Grandpa Rudys.

To the amazingly talented Marta Kissi, who made my characters appear out of thin air. Your magical artwork brought Thomas and Chip and company to life in ways I never could have imagined. Standing ovation!

To my family—Scott, Paige, Weston, and Rand—who let me drag them to terrible magic shows, and who support my crazy ideas and my mostly complete sentences, and who always let me take the curtain call as if I did it all on my own. Alacazam!